Prasvapa

Chand Svare Ghei

Prasvapa

Chand Svare Ghei

Short Stories

First edition © Chand Svare Ghei 2015

Graphic design:
Chand Svare Ghei
Cover photo:
Sonata Jaseliunaite
Photographs:
Edition Cumulus
Illustrations:
Katarina Sand Midtlyng
Distribusjon:
www.chasvag.com

This is a self-published publication.
www.chasvag.com e-mail: don_chand@chasvag.com

ISBN 978-82-998681-8-1 (printed)
ISBN 978-82-998681-9-8 (e-book)

प्रस्वाप

prasvāpa – of consciousness during sleep

Special thanks to:
Jan Håvard Bleka for trying to proof-read UK English.
Sonata Jaseliunaite for the cover photo.
Edition Cumulus for the photographs.
Katarina Sand Midtlyng for the illustrations.
Klaus Tvedt for the introduction.
Laura Standen for proof-reading and linguistic support.
Casteau Scribblers (www.casteau-scribblers.com) for feedback, inspiration, advice and corrections.
Drew Wagar for inspiration.

Thanks to:
Bjørn, Stephan, Steinar, Cecilie, Bernard, Jarl Yngve, Vivian, Kim, Vivi, Eric, Liyanne, Sissel, Warry, Patrick, Tom Erik, Vigdis, Johnny, Tommy, Klaus, Silje, Turid, Agnieszka, 2xSebastian, John Erik, Harm, Kari Elisabeth, Sada, Tez, Janine, Woo, Sven, Helge, Mikjel, Øystein, Henriette, Øygunn, Raquel, Harald, Richard, Sigurd, Kjetil, Freddy, Renate, Vidar, Elin, Lina, Kenneth, Gunn, Linda, Miltos, Robert, Mark, 2xHilde, Jürgen, Jarle, Melina, Morten, Marius, Enzo, Astrid, Miroslaw, 2xDavid, Graeme, Joseph, Renee, Rozemarijn, Kai, Bjørnulf, Arne Martin, Gunn Marit, Stein Kjetil, the town of Vyskov and Hans.

Introduction

Dear Brother! Dear Readers!

When opening this book I can almost guarantee that you will experience something special. For he is special, my brother. He is running where other do not dare to walk, howling where others are afraid to utter a single word. That's just the way he is. Special.

Of course I am saying this because he is my brother. But the truth is – if there is such a thing – that he always has been different. You could probably say there was no way to avoid it. He stood out in the rather homogenic crowd in seventies Norway. And it didn't help that our small family wasn't very conventional either. We could have been mistaken for a travelling circus when settling in the countryside outside of Trondheim. And in some ways we were. I think we were seen as foreigners, strangers not really able to blend in, not really meant to be there, and as of such, we were treated like that. This experience, I think, can be felt in – and in between – the lines of everything my brother has written.

My brother always said that it was I who should have become the writer in our family. I do not agree. Even though I had the abilities to express myself, to write, at an early age it was always he who had the most vivid imagination. Even as a child I can remember how he charmed the grownups immensely with his absurd and wild stories that he made up on the spot.

A more mature and darker side of these fantasies come to life in these short stories. A stark contrast to the professional life he leads as an IT and telecommunications engineer. A rebellion perhaps? Literature as a place where the darkness runs free and violence becomes tangible, though there is always some light seeping in through the window. Throughout these short stories I can feel a strong will to communicate. That's what writing really is all about, the urge to tell stories and convey experiences, and that is why, I believe, he became the author and I didn't.

I will never become a neutral reader of these stories. Yes, I do have a degree in the science of literature, but most and foremost I am Chand Svare Ghei's brother. I cannot read a single line of these stories without seeing him before me. Even though the stories are about – at least mostly – fictive matters, for me they bring to life memories of our childhood and adolescence, they bring to life the primitive instinct of protecting him.

As a child I always ran after everyone who harmed him or did try to harm him, because I already then, at a very early age, understood that he was different, in many ways very different, and I knew that he did experience that every day.

Today one of the things I appreciate most about my brother is that he stands out from the crowd, that he is so strange, weird, crazy, whimsical, nondescript and unpredictable, that he is being himself. I am glad he does.

Congratulations with yet another book!

Klaus Tvedt
8 October 2015

An everyday adventure

"In this chaotic world of decadence and demise, it is difficult to keep a pure hope to still believe in true love."

A lush flutter of trees wept out centuries of events woven with each colour hidden within the floating leaves. Tales, stories and even the local myths retold and modified to fit the size of the beholder. As if the weather and the outdoors tried to outperform her indoor silence.

Sadness wore her; you had to be an expert to notice it on her appearance. She tucked away any item or object that remised untidiness. Washed out the entire house till it shone without a spot. A wooden scent of Pine-Sol, almost alive, emanated from the floors.

She lit candles in various sizes around the house; flames flashed over the built-in darkness, wonderfully comforting her vigorously.

This was her home, her sanctuary, and this was where she found her peace. Not alone, but in harmony with nature. Distant enough from the nearest neighbour to never meet people when she did not intend to.

She played her favourite Bel Canto CD, *Shimmering, Warm & Bright* and read one of her favourite gems of a book, Gustav Meyrink's *The Golem*.

The agony from her troubled past still lingered inside, but the wounds were no longer gaping holes. Not even the worst part, her trip to the Netherlands, where she once had been tricked into aborting the only child she had ever borne.

A troublesome memory, a nightmare of lying stuck on a bench, with white suited medical personnel around her resembling an alien abduction. Waking up from a deep sleep, realising the unexplainable, the impossible. When she arrived in the country she had been two, in love; she returned transformed, lost, broken and alone.

In her pocket she wore an Apache Tear, a stone that allegedly helped her deal with the torment that overflowed what a single person can handle. With time the grief converted her life into one of solace.

I always believed the world to be a better place. Possibly naïve. But what would the world be without innocence? My guess, pretty close to a concentrated lump of all the extremities of terrible substances it contains.

As much as I would wish not to experience the obstacles in my life, nobody should have to endure such. I now understand, it's just too common. Yet I refuse to become hard and cynical, and let the darkness win.

Does it make me a hypocrite, because I choose to lock the world out, to become a loner? Maybe, but it's the best I can do. I did not survive well out there, and I am unable to bear that life anymore.

I might not be able to save the world, but I can try to save myself.

Her cat, Deniz, came jumping on her lap, desperately wanting attention. Such delight a small animal brought into her world. Rumour had it that having a pet might increase your health significantly. While she was not one for science, she felt that Deniz had brought her more pleasure in life than any man ever did. But more importantly, it was pure, non-craving joy.

Here, time could be twisted around its regularity at any pace desired, like nothing actually mattered. Pages of a book, a nice cup of homemade herb tea, and the meow of a cat passed into memories without even noticing.

Much like every day and every week would pass. The pleasures in the small events; a kind of life that eventually had the potential to harvest something new.

And it did not even matter if it didn't.

This Sunday was no different until Deniz rapidly jumped out of her lap and ran away, meowing like crazy. Was she suddenly that hungry?

She got up, needing to prevent ripples in paradise, and an everyday adventure had begun. Running after Deniz, not to the food bowl, but to the main house door, her personal portal to society, to chaos.

She detested opening it; not now, not this late. She was tempted to turn back to the safety of her cosy chair. But hey, the cat pawed the bottom of the door, convincing her to submit to her cat's control.

The force of the wind panicked her when the door swung fully open. A few leaves found their way inside before she placed herself outside. Deniz led a trail in front of her.

Like a marionette, she become enthralled to follow this mysterious behaviour. The teasing occurrence of the autumn; what would happen next?

An appealing scenery: the last rays of sunshine reflected over the colourful landscape and slightly reminded her of magic.

After ten minutes of strolling aside the road, it started to snow. In five minutes the colourful spectacle of autumn transformed into the tranquil peace of winter white.

Her life had become magic.

She spotted it immediately. An intruder.

A man, if he even could be called that. A lump of human living flesh, dumped in the gutter, like the drunken bum he was.

My first impression was to leave him there to rot. Why should I care about this stranger? But then why would Deniz care for him? What was he doing here? After all, he was a man, and I don't like men. I don't particularly like people. But then again, if I ignored him, I would be no better than the world I loathe.

He was clearly a soul that suffered, in his own way. Comparable to me, he wore his own wounds more on the inside than for public view.

I need to take care of him. Take him home and get him on his feet. Later when he gets better, I can throw him back to the wolves. Yes, that is what I will do.

The change of days were imminent. Now they were three – two humans and one cat – conditions had to evolve. They always do.

In the beginning he was so weak, not only by physical condition, but also from within – something he wore, a pain he could not endure. Natural progression demanded him to inherit the Apache Tear.

A classical scenario: girl helps man onto his feet, with the help of a loving feline.

But over time, he would walk, talk and help with the small chores around and outside the house. The pressure of time, people or even performance didn't exist. It was simple days of life and interaction.

Laughter filled the location, lively days with pleasure. Growing closer, like a family. Seeds of something new sprung out of a new life.

I had given up hope. I did not believe anymore. Why would I? Never, ever in my experience had I witnessed that it could be true. That it could be real. How this poverty had deluded me into this, and yet eventually it happened.

I never will throw this man out to the wolves. I grow to care for him more every day.

No matter what you experience in life, what you have to endure, there is exclusively one real satisfaction: the one of true love.

To kill a Christmas tree

"The vast difference and distance from us

do not mean they don't feel pain."

There are about 2.4 billion Christians in the world. Each Christmas they need a tree – to stand erected and proud, to illuminate and cover gifts for a few holy days before they throw it away.

"Look out at the sky, the stars are so bright today." Dad pointed with his right hand. We pressed our heads and noses to the partially iced-up kitchen window and let the marvel of a clear, dark evening hustle over us. The celestial objects, so remote that they are impossible to comprehend, blinked and shone in competitive harmony. The spectacle of blinking patterns reminded us of the earliest and most eternal forms of art. A moment of awe; these kinds of moments kept our sanity away from the reality at hand. Poverty.

We never had a lot of money. We never had much of anything but time. Strangely, as meagre as our lives were, they were abundant with niceties such as waiting, listening to silence and discovering the music of nothing. Throw me a busy life with a plethora of money anytime, and later, much later, I got that.

We consumed a meal of fish sticks and potatoes. I think probably my childhood consisted mostly of that: potatoes in all flavours and always fish sticks. How I hated fish sticks, but they are cheap and provided us with a hot meal on the table.

When I reflect on the past there are two things that stand out as monuments; the first one was the constant hunger. I was so skinny that my ribs became my distinguishing body feature. The second one was the tranquillity; time seemed to pass so slowly that everything was at a standstill.

Dad had a past as someone prominent at IBM, someone with money, power and a future, and he had left it all behind to be with Mum, to be with us. Dad would never discuss his past; he would brush away questions with a joke or use the opportunity to change the subject to something in the present.

Even today I have no idea – possibly for the better.

My father was a kind of replica of my mother; what I mean is that it seemed that he did not really have a mind or life of his own, but did whatever she wanted, more like a servant than a man. But for a kid, that is excellent news; as a consequence he had plenty of time being a plaything for young kids.

My mum was the craziest, caring woman I have ever known. She could create anything with her hands. She made the most peculiar dolls, hats and clothes. These skills proved to be handy for providing us and friends with the strangest Christmas gifts. With no false modesty, I will claim that she saved many a person's Christmas just with her outgoing and modest nature and the weirdness of her presents.

Most of the year, when there was no Christmas, she would still make hoards of strange creations and surprise us with the most remarkable homemade toys.

To sum it up, it was a bizarre but wonderful childhood.

While we let our minds wander through the light years of space, Mum would bring us back to the warm odour of boiled potatoes and proclaim that we did not have enough money to buy a Christmas tree this year.

When the early dinner was over, I went out to catch the last opportunity of the day to play with the snow together with my brother, Helge, who was four years older than me. My parents would answer my born curiosity with answers like: "It is like this so you can have something to ask about." Or even worse: "Just because it is." But Helge knew everything and understood how to answer pretty much any question I threw at him.

As much as my parents tried to be there for us, they were in fact a pair of grown kids; they did not *know* how to be the adults we needed. Often they were more childish than us; to compensate for that I had Helge and Helge had nobody.

Out there in the early darkness, digging further in our snow cave, I asked him what we should do when without a Christmas tree. Could it really be Christmas without one?

The snow cave was mostly dug with our hands and had several corridors and small rooms where we would leave a banana or a mandarin to freeze, later to eat real-fruit sorbet.

"What if we steal a tree, cut it down ourselves? What do you say?" was the suggestion Helge threw at me.

"Are you sure it's not dangerous?" was my insecure answer.

"Of course it is dangerous, but we can do it. Think how happy it will make Mummy." I got caught in the temptation; it was meant to be.

We snuck into the shed and borrowed an axe and set out on an expedition to find a nice Christmas tree, somewhere where nobody could watch us. The trail took us many hours. We were both tired and exhausted when we finally came to a small place, far away from people – darkness coming faster; a few young trees smiling. It had a green cover against the enchanting, covering snowflakes.

My feet grew cold, a tingling freeze burn in my toes.

"There it is, our tree." A cold winter glove pointed at a young green Picea abies. Such a true statement: a tree, perfectly formed, with a green colour that hurt our eyes against the shades of white. We both knew it to be true and jumped up and down the best we could, sinking further and further into the pale desert, forming a dent.

Helge swung the axe with a mighty force. A child's blow, but it still counted.

Screams of pain and despair hit me. The tree spoke to me: "Why me, why do you chop me down?" All the other trees around looked angry at me. But there was no real noise, no actual change around us. In our triumph I was filled with sadness, grief for our tree, a life wasted for no other reason than vanity among the penniless.

The more sceptical would probably think it must have been my imagination. But I can tell you: for me it was such an intense experience that even today I shiver when I recollect the excruciating horror.

It only happened to me this once; soon it was over and we dragged our prize with us back home, creating a nice, large trail. The return trip turned us into nerve wrecks. We had to transport the tree all the way home without being spotted. Neatly, the evening was upon us and it assisted us in becoming extended shadows of the winter queen.

Back at our place we left the tree outside and stepped in to tell our parents the good news. In the hallway, as we were throwing the wet and cold clothes off our bodies, Mum came storming at us with glowing eyes. Happy eyes, such eyes of joy I had not seen for quite some time. Dad ran up just behind her and he lifted Helge and me up in the air.

She screamed joyfully: "We got a free tree as a gift from the Heidallers, can you believe it?"

It was a moment of family joy and hidden shame. Disappointingly, Helge backed out from the whole deal. That night I snuck out, alone, after bedtime, dragging the five-year-old tree behind me, covered by darkness, with the moon as my witness.

I located a decent remote location and left the tree there, lost and alone. We stole many hundred years of possible stout and proud years from it, for dubious reasons.

Standing there on that night, dark, full of fairy tales, within a vast and cold universe, I went through a mental metamorphosis. For the first time in my life I shed a tear, whose warmth tingled in a line down my face.

I sensed deep in my heart that I never would cry again.

Kenneth Johansen — hideaway

"The brutality of reality is that sometimes simple and done deals become convoluted over time."

It seemed that Kenneth and Birger had been friends forever, that every single case and crime thrown at them was nothing but petty change for their clue-solving capabilities. But it was a charade; in reality they were stuck in a dirty world, where luck was their best weapon, and luck can last for only so long.

The day's best parts passed and slowly gave way to its darker sister. Inside the establishment sat Kenneth with his best friend and partner in crime-fighting, Birger, around a small table, each with half a litre of beer. Although he lived a life where alcohol was second in his nature, he did not drink often anymore. This time was no different; the plan was to get that *one* beer down and then get home.

Unsettling feelings blazed through both of them. The latest case had been at a standstill for two months and they both realised that future prognoses contained no wonderful surprises.

They had been involved in stalemates before; the difference this time was that they still had found no way to untie the knots. Maybe this one turned out to be their first utter failure. One time has to be the first; that does not make it easier to swallow.

"There is one way we can break this case, but you will not fancy it." Kenneth rose slightly on his seat and put his right arm up to Birger's collar.

Birger did not yet comprehend the situation and babbled away. "Yeah, right. You have some stupid idea bubbling up, one we did not consider yet, which suddenly will—"

Kenneth didn't let him finish, but pulled his finger slightly to the collar. "It's not a stupid idea, but it's an idea that will repulse you." Kenneth moved his face closer to Birger. His eyes were similar to two growing bulbs gazing into him with mad importance.

Birger looked closely into those abasing eyes; this was serious. "Tell me, then, how you want to blow this."
"Sara."

Silence can be many things, but often silence is the subjective opinion of one or more minds. The two friends were surrounded by a growing silence, and they both felt awkward. Birger mimicked Kenneth's earlier movements with his left arm and let his grip tighten around his collar. "You mean, *that* Sara?"

Kenneth quietly nodded.

Both men held each other by the throats and gazed angrily into each other's eyes while the distance between their faces grew shorter and shorter. Soon it would be just eyes to eyes and nothing else. The tone of Birger's voice changed to a rusty can rolling down a playground slide. "Never! I don't understand how you can even suggest this. We both remember what happened, and she can't ever be again. She is a no-discussion item and we need to keep it that way. I consider this conversation closed. And you will never mention her again."

Anger poured out of Birger like never before. His kind and nice friend became a furious steam machine running on Starbucks. He tried to wiggle out of the grip and leave the place, but Kenneth held him back, keeping his voice low and with controlled nicety. "Consider it. Even though we know the mistakes of the past, it has become a long time ago. Even the hardest rocks corrode with time; nothing is absolute, and if you leave room for that train of thought, you'll soon realise what she is: the perfect person to help us get back in the game. To open some doors, the right ones to close the case. This case is not just some small-time burglary, but about people who need us more to execute than to sit down and grieve."

The objective illusion of silence became complete. Second after second passed. There was about zero movement between the partners, but compensation came by high-speed thoughts and feelings passing through the axon train stations. The voice lost most of its strength. "Fine, but this one is on you. I want nothing to do with this."

This time Kenneth let Birger wiggle off. He finished up his glass in one go before he left the establishment.

पूरस्वाप

When Kenneth finally made it home, Live waited with a now-cold dinner; it was her special version of spaghetti aglio olio scampi. A simple dish, but hard to master. She would fry olive oil with cut garlic on a low temperature while the spaghetti cooked, and just at the end she would raise the heat a little and add the scampi. Then she would mix it all together and sprinkle freshly ground salt and pepper over it.

Today it tasted perfect, but in all dismay it was the only thing that was so. It was easy for her to grasp the wrongness in him. Not that he would not have his share of plenty shitty days, but today it was different, crappier, or something else, than usual.

Live hated it; she appreciated the simple life they used to have. Just him and her, far out in the countryside; days would pass each other, but nobody or nothing would rush it. Days passed by for them to relish each other, and despite the wounds inside, they used to be happier. It was the life she longed for, the life she was made for.

But then she had made the mistake of inviting him for a weekend in Oslo, and Kenneth had met the long, hauling arms of his past, and decided to stay. To return to the special unit, which people called Ramlösa after the Swedish mineral water.

She had moved with him and ended up having to share him, not with other women, but with a job that demanded too much of him. He looked up at her, relished her and told her the food was fantastic just to finish up with the rather bony information that he needed to leave for an extended time.

She peeked back at him with female despair. "Damn it, Kenneth! Haven't you done enough? Do you believe you can save the world all by yourself? We both know the first time you joined Ramlösa you were optionless, but this time around it is your choice. Can you not ease up, reduce your commitment to work, in such a way that we could spend more time together?"

Kenneth looked down to the three leftover lines of pasta, kept cosy

34

by a small scampi. "I am sorry. I realise I work too much, too often. But someone needs to do it, and this someone is me with a little help from Birger."

She laughed, convincing nobody. "But you are not even very good at what you do."

He chuckled back. "Don't tell anybody, but now that I hardly drink anymore, there is not really anything I am good at. But this job is the only thing I know."

पूरस्वाप

In regards of the spectrum of possibilities that life provided, only one activity lay close to Birger's heart: cruising, driving and losing himself to the false pretension that the speed limit actually was any fast.

With a heavy heart he had traded his Escort for a Fiesta, a sad downgrade in his eyes, even though he secretly referred to his vehicle as a Ford Ferrari. Still a secret even if Kenneth knew.

It was trouble in Birger's senses, thoughts and behaviours. A tickling sensation – the bad kind – rummaging throughout his body. Sara. A person he believed never to face again.

Not purely the thought about her, though, who she had been, what she had done, but also the betrayal; Kenneth's betrayal burned as deep in him as if he actually had a soul.

Why would Kenneth, his best and probably only friend, the one who understood him all too well, go against him in this way? Any other person in the world, yes, but never, ever, Sara. In his opinion, she did not even deserve the gift of life.

Birger knew he would not get any answers, and not anything else either. The only thing that might soothe him was enduring speed on endless roads – the mean streak hitting him in its regular rhythm – till the point of exhaustion and ending up sleeping in the car on the side of the road. What a life, or what had life eventually provided him?

Raga Rockers pulled hard riffs from his speakers, screaming about meaningless days passing by and of cameras hidden in the clouds. Every happening is registered and analysed. Birger wondered what the one above thought about him, Kenneth and Sara.

पूरस्वाप

Thirty thousand feet is nothing, nothing in the measures of space and infinity, but for Kenneth it felt like some kind of torture. Being away from mother earth, far, far away in a tin box, throwing itself at mad speeds around, without knowing where or what. How little was needed to take his presumably safe seat into a horrific situation, which in the end would lead to the death of him and all the surrounding strangers.

Needless to say, he was scared shitless. First one, then two, then more JDs with Coke to be emptied on a half-full stomach.

It had always been Karianne who had been his true love, but nevertheless, Live was the one who made the cure to his chaotic life. A cruel joke hangs above the fact that the one he wanted was lost forever, and the one he had, who cherished him and loved him, he chose to slip away from, similar to the slow dripping of crude oil.

It was said that time would heal all wounds, but the memory of

Karianne was covered in the eternal stench of bitter agony. The liquid he poured into himself had the clever feature of taking over at a certain moment, easing the pain and easing the suffering, like rain falling down a bottomless well.

It was what he needed and, at the same time, the one thing he essentially should stay away from, his wicked guardian, the addiction to Lord Alcohol and his ragged followers.

He had never been a social drinker and, at the time of landing, he would rather stay seated, with the rest of the plane supplies. He somehow managed to force himself downstairs, through baggage control. He wiped off the white marker on his luggage, grabbed a taxi and there he was: New Delhi.

The place you go to hide away.

Alcohol and heat have never been the best of friends, and he needed to find a location away from the noise bombs created by hoards of people, rickshaws, bicycles, cars and holy cows. To a pub, where men, and only men, sat unhappily at tables covered in indelicate smoke fumes and drank terrible Kingfisher beer.

How sad a spot for any other man than him; here he could be alone in the group and be free to nurture his inner demons in a country where holiness could be found on every tile. Till such a point that he would lose himself, drop and be the happy offer to any scavenging creep.

"Kenneth?"

The place you go to be found.

पुरस्वाप

37

"So let me see if I've got this right. You are stuck on a case at home, with an organisation, or let's say more a mafia, comprising only girls. With the lack of progress, in fact with consecutive months of zero progress, your idea is to find a woman, a special one, to infiltrate the environment. And the single person on this bulb you believe in is me?" Sara gave it a mild laugh.

They sat in her apartment. Her maid was preparing lunch, a selection of Indian dishes, with her utmost care. Kenneth was rusty, not just because of the withdrawal of the hooks of his lord, but also because the situation felt so unreal. Deep inside him, he had never actually believed that he would face Sara again. "Yes."

"And are you sure? That the actual reason you are here is not because you wanted to see me?" She rose up and walked closer to him.

"Never, Sara. I would never have come if we did not need you, and yes, in this case I comprehend that you are the only one who can perform this duty, and you know just as well why." Kenneth rose up as well and turned around to face away from her.

"Tell me why," she said, getting awfully close to him.

He avoided her and moved against the window. Out there he could almost sense the nausea of a world gone mad, the world he needed to shield himself from. "I loved only a single person in my life; it was her, and you, you know what you did. If you could do that, then you are the right person for this job. Men can make some terrible mafias, but a mafia comprising women, that is the most gruesome thing I have ever encountered. Each individual in the mafia carries the consolidated hate of every male misdeed since the first apple bite. Have a look at the file on the table and you will understand why this is more important than our feelings towards each other."

She listened to him, took up the folder and started reading. He smuggled himself around to peek at her. Her strong lines flowing through her body, the tight blouse that threatened to break from the pressure of her small breasts. How was it possible that she still looked the same after all these years? What secrets of life had she discovered in this divine capital? When she was finished with an initial scan and moved towards him again, his eyes were again deeply involved with exterior matters. She got so close to him that the warmth of her breath blew in his ear. "And what is in it for me?"

He felt her arms closing around him, finding his stomach and soothing it. "To be honest, I don't know. If I came here because of this case, or if I am here because of you, it should be an easy answer, but everything is much more complex than I wish it to be."

Both stood by the window like a lovely couple, both looking outside for signs of hope. "I will do it."

He turned around, their lips so near to each other that their breaths crashed. Eye to eye, so close it seemed as three of them – a spiritual third eye. Her eyes shone as a blue shining snow crystal.

"Let's go, we have some unfinished business to attend to."

I believe in magic

"I can smell wizardry from miles away."

Desolate ruins, the odour of decay, rot and even death. A lonesome girl, not yet a woman, stood alone, screaming. Could it be that she was not entirely abandoned? Maybe there is a gentleman, a hero or villain, closing in on her? And if it weren't for magic, nobody would have any idea what might happen.

"Dave, where are you? Dave?" It was a nasal repeated scream.

Dave ran towards the ruins, heading straight to the source from which the sound emanated. "I am here," his voice screeched almost breathless; it consisted more of puffs than vocals.

"No, I am searching for Dave." She was looking desperate in any direction possible, but never at Dave.

"I am Dave." He repeated it a few times, but to no avail. She was desperately looking for him and repeatedly asked for him with her almost childish voice.

He took a step closer to her, with his head just in front; her blonde hair was flowing in the air, even when there was no wind. Her pale blue eyes shone of tenacious and immediate desperation. "Look here, Your Highness, I am Dave. I am standing straight in front of you; knock it off." But again, it had little or no effect on her. He slapped her head with his left hand. It provided him immersive release to slap Her Highness silly.

Fuming anger filled Dave, but there was naught he could do. An idea flowered inside his brain cells. "Would you like me to help you find Dave?"

"Yes, please, that would be nice. We need to find Dave." For the first time she looked at him; the pupils seemed large and frightened and not able to properly lock on him.

"Tell me from the beginning what happened." His voice had become friendlier, almost pleasant.

She took him literally and started telling him. "You see, my father, the king, wanted to send me away, in secret – how overwhelmingly indecent. It was the gruesome Grand Mage Elevor who was expected on a surprise visit. The secluded reason was that my father – need I remind you he is the king after all? – suspected that the Grand Mage brewed a scrupulous plan to force-marry me. Can you imagine me becoming the wife of such a savage? I mean, yes, he is an executor of the finer arts of the very fabric of our universe, but he is hideous, smells dirty and ancient rumours say he is a thousand years old. But the worst thing is, he is close to bald; you just can't trust a bald mage, that's something we all know. No, give me a valiant prince with pride, honour and a dignified posture, that is what I need." Her irises flicked from side to side, never meeting anything to rest on. "Evidently, I had no wish to leave; I prefer the cushy life of a city, a place where important ladies like me can find purpose, pursue the delights of a higher society and sophisticated scandals to slander about."

She held her hands, hanging down by force, as if she pretended to be caught up in a straitjacket.

"As my travel was to be covert, our party would be light: a horse carrier, a jockey and my detail. I was assigned only one person to take care of my safety – what an outrageous decision – and it was no ordinary knight, but that weasel of an upcoming champion, Knight Dave of Worthingsworth. I mean, who does he think he is? Everybody knows that his house lost its worth a century ago and lingers on an old debt from the crown. He doesn't even address me in the correct manner, but bullies me around like I was a commoner. He is pure muscle and machine, but brain, not so much. That rat of—"

Dave grew tired of having to listen to rubbish talk in that high-pitched voice. "Tell me, my lady, when and where did you lose Dave?"

She paid little notice to the interruption, except her pupils continued to grow like small moons. "It was an ambush. The carriage was not much to talk about: uncomfortable, ordinary, low standard and pitiful. I detested it, kept inside the wagon to myself, and tried to somehow survive those harsh conditions. When we hit the outskirts of the capital and were about to enter the exotic forest of Fiutsui, the attack emerged, swiftly like a morning brew."

Occasionally her whole body twitched.

"Out of a small ruin, which had seen its glory in a long-forgotten age, came the sneaking bastards, hoards of them. Ridiculously bad odds for us; it would be easier to win the lottery. Our nameless driver, or at least I never took the effort to learn his name, got killed in that same moment with an arrow piercing his neck. It's better not to know people who die, then there is no need to feel sorry for them."

She moved her feet a little, as if she found the ground to be unstable. "Dave the Brave came about and slung his monstrous sword around him, a madman in distress. He was a berserker fulfilling his purpose: bloodshed of the first degree. The sword extended him brutally to slash the enemy in bits and pieces."

As if her hands were wounded, she lifted them both up and swung around, to describe the hacking and slashing.

"How many did he wound and eventually end the life of? I have no idea, too many. Nobody was able to stop him, a terrible inhuman whirlwind. The stench, the fragance of fresh blood squirting in every direction, the slices of inner body parts pulsating with their last fragments of life, and let us not forget excrement. I mean, I pride myself never to gag, to vomit, but then I couldn't help myself."

This reminded Dave to pay attention to the rueful scent around him; even though it had been lingering there for a while, he choked.

The eminent lady did not notice, and continued blabbering. "Swordplay – what a crude way of fighting, how naked and dishonourable it makes us people, like fake tomato meatballs to eat for an informal dinner. Same I say about medicine, these blunt instruments they use to mend our sophisticated limbs are so barbaric. No, give me instead a magician—"

"Bloody hell, I am allergic to magic—" Dave shivered at the thought.

Dave was upset, not just a little, but even repulsed. Here, directly in front of him, this lady, this princess, badmouthed him, his life and events; she was a bitch. He desired to slap her silly, if only she had not been of such high birth; he barely managed to refrain.

An infant chuckle. "How curious, so was Dave, this small, sturdy fighter. Oh, wait a minute! I have to tell you something, but promise not to tell Dave, ok?" Without waiting for an answer she continued. "I must say that despite me not fancying violence particularly much, I find Dave to be quite handsome, and there he fought a small army of enemy combatants all by himself; even the king's first knight could not beat such a feat. I am humbly impressed and slightly interested in knowing him better. Such a man can both be a good friend, and possibly something more. Alas, the winning streak had to stop when the traitor, the Grand Mage Elevor, made his gallant entry and blew a fireball against us. Dave coughed and coughed, allergic as he was."

She kept her hands up high, waving them as an excited, little girl. "An immersive ball of fire, heat and light hit us. The wagon, with me inside it, blew to pieces. Dave's eyes were running, but he simply refused to stop, refused to let the allergy best him, and he was running his fastest towards the wizard. He kept his sword up high, not able to see much through his crying eyeballs. The distance was far enough for the mage to send some pretty nasty spells at Dave: magic missiles, lightning bolts and even the tremor of earth, all of which heavily affected Dave, slowed him down, hurt and drained his health. But still, Dave refused to give up."

Immersed by her own excitement, she did a few small jumps.

"Time elapsed slowly as a turtle's dinner tale; he was finally at his destination and since the mage never anticipated Dave would actually make the stretch, no magic shield had been made. The ancient sword cut his body like maple syrup. The Grand Mage screeched a hollow scream, the concluding one of pure hate, evil and death."

Dave became slightly relaxed and happy; it was not usual for him to receive this kind of praise, and on this occasion from a royal. In the desolate place they stayed, time seemed to work in uneven ways and now it was almost seeping to a slow-motion halting. In the distance, the sound of flapping wings – a dragonfly, surrounded by a magical eerie, came flying.

The princess immediately got struck with terror, as the direct translation of dragonfly in her own native language was "eye stinger". She firmly believed it was there to sting her eyes out.
It was a special spectacle; the light surrounding it displayed a variety of changing hues and colours, and somehow the princess sensed that the dragonfly meant no danger. It flew to the now silent couple and landed on her shoulder.

The light radiated and grew into a ball. The incrementing globe of charming luminance swallowed them both.

Suddenly, the princess laughed, but this time it was different, adolescent and majestic. "Oh, Dave, there you are. I have been looking for you all over the place. I am so happy to see you." She opened her arms, jumped into him and gave him a good, close and informal hug. Dave did not have time to jump back in surprise and got smooched all over by Her Highness. It was the embrace with the smell of lavender. Lavender reminded him of his boyhood years, a young girl called Anne, and it comforted and delighted him. He wished it would last forever, but in reality it took only a few seconds.

The dragonfly left the couple with determined wing flaps, leaving a trail of glamorous coloured lights, its mission now complete.

Despite being a knight, Dave tried to man himself up. "Your Majesty, I am so happy to see you alive; if it hadn't been for my darn allergy, I should have saved us from that darn fireball as well."

The princess laughed again; her voice was now back to its full strength and filled the open space as if she owned it. "You are not really allergic to magic; it is probably just something you made up in your head. Did you really think you could butcher thirty warriors by yourself?"

Dave sheathed his sword and raised his arms and grunted some words in his defence before she continued.

"You might not know it, but I am a long-time devoted student of the arts of sorcery. I supported your carnage with a few nice spells: haste, protection, perception and rage. It was a chance, of course, but without it, I dare say you would be a dead man and I would be captured for a leading role in an enforced marriage."

Dave chewed out more incomprehensible words before he started laughing. Soon they were both laughing as they realised they were quite the team; they dared to embrace once more. Despite their difficulties, unbelievable odds and even their own internal issues, they had endured and won. With the wagon, food and belongings they knew they still had challenges before them, but cared little about them. In fact, they could prove a promise of another adventure.

On the run

"'Crime never pays' is commonly sold as fact, but truth shows us otherwise; the majority of cases are left unsolved."

It was a dry summer day, with a blowing wind filling the air with dust. A lonely man tracks downhill an excuse of a road, his mind filling him with lust and longing. One step at a time, tiresome and slow to ensure the maximum output of his own reserves. Grudging over something, an incident that happened recently, causes him pain.

"Do you want a lift?" she shouted. The Landrover's tires screeched the sand beneath them and the door opened. Inside was a girl, naturally alluring, like from a famous soda water commercial.

"Instead, you should say, 'you wanna ride?' It sounds better." He laughed, took a few steps and jumped into the car.

Once they were tucked inside, the vehicle moved again.

"I fancy it here. Maybe we can stay here for a longer time?" she more than suggested.

It was both the right and wrong time to tell her the news. "Events have been triggered already, and we need to move from this place soon, probably within two weeks."

The brakes again. She looked straight at him, eyes flaring. "What do you mean, in two weeks?"

She was such a captivating sight. It was hard for him to keep his posture. Her chestnut brown, thin, but lively hair felt so flat; it could almost be a mirror. Her dark eyes were shining, with a hint of purple.

"When one is on the run there are two unwritten laws that will always lead to a repeated outcome. First, if you had some status in the world of crime, the local crime boss will always take a direct interest in you. Letting you into his future plans and performing not so secret meetings with the two of you. The second unwritten law is that this in turn will make several of his higher staff jealous." He laughed and continued. "The number one for example is the big guy with the muscles, who has been led to believe that he'll be the inheritor of…" Holding his eyes to hers made it easier to concentrate, it made everything simple.

She broke away. "Janus, you mean?"

"Yes, in this case we are talking about Janus. And Janus will never be the next on the throne, at least not for long, but he believes so; that's what keeps him faithful. But yes, I recently had a run in with him, one of those where he needed to blow off his jealousy and show some muscle. That's a clear indication that things will get worse. So, the outcome is, when you're on the run, you stay on the run. You never stay at the same place for long."

The car was moving again, but inside it, they found a pressing silence, until she cracked it, saying, "And how long are we going to be on the run?"

Her train of thoughts overwhelmed him. She was the jewel in his life. He looked at her and smiled. Even though they were in motion, he put his hands on hers, and she gave him a glimpse of a smile back.

He had never known love this profound, so deep, full of compassion, but with no requirements, just free. It had changed him, from an inverted, self-loathing criminal who deeply hated life to a man with a future. But he knew that if he wanted that future, he had to grab it and change his everyday life.

They were trying to find that new life, by leaving the old one. The problem was, the law would not let them off the hook that easy. Yet he understood how difficult it would be for her to be constantly on the move. In their deep affection, they had both agreed on the strenuous way to the new hope. Did she, now, deep into the mist, regret it?

She stopped the Landrover again, to reflect on more important matters, full embracing, while whispering, "I'm sorry, I always realised the challenge. It's just that I'm falling in love with this place; it contains that dreamy peace I believe we both are longing for, so I hoped to stay."

He countered dryly, "I love you. And nothing, let it be stars, monsters or the most terrible crime lords you might imagine, can stop me from being with you, always."

पूरस्वाप

Nightmares. Nightmares had always followed him through the

world like long-lost nagging friends you did not really want to see around. But this night, he had a calm dream. Vast moors as far as the eye perceived; the sun flickering its rays through it. It was a dream of love. A couple, him and her, running naked to the other side, where only God stood witness. It was a dream of freedom.

It was easy to understand what he needed to do when awakening griped its reality finger at his consciousness. But first he looked to the right of him and glanced at the sleeping beauty beside him.

Before, life had been not simply a struggle to survive, but pain, constant agony. The world was not meant to be this way, a place of devastation, uselessness, with no meaning, just survival. Sigbjørn Obstfelder had always been right. He did not belong here.

He did not grasp what had happened to him when she entered his life, but it was the change, the miracle, everybody was dreaming of, but exclusively left for the lucky ones to experience. It was the realisation of dreams coming true.

And he had gone through a metamorphosis; he realised that he did not desire life to continue in his old ways, the one of a forever medium-time criminal. There were two choices: to rat or to run. She had begged him to rat, but deep down, there was something, a sense of futile *Godfather* pride that told him it was the wrong choice.

He regretted it now. A life on the run had proven to be even worse than what he was running from. But his dream gave him a new idea to pursue. Hope.

पूरस्वाप

Karl overlooked the office as if he was a tired Garfield copy. His plump fingers drew through his short, white hair to signify that once there had been plenty to show off to girls. Blood-stricken eyes told the tale of light insomnia. It was the body of a man whom life had treated well, in such amounts that he could afford to waste his own wealth.

Tobias' eyes stared intensively at the infamous creatures on the desk in front of him: small scorpions with tiny claws and a tail, alive, deadly and ready to strike at any time. "Unlike other crime lords, whose claims of fame include such feats as ripping out a man's heart and eating it or skinning a man alive, which is an arousing set-up to create fear, I, on the other hand, have these highly trained murderous scorpions that will kill any enemy of mine."

A roaring laughter, from someone with half a neck, filled the room, before he continued.

"Would you care for a demonstration?"

Without waiting for an answer, Karl screamed, "Attention!"

The nine scorpions moved, crawled, and within three seconds, they were formed in the pattern of a platoon, with the commander in front. Saluting. "Perform parade!" The command was executed immediately and immaculately. The horrifying scorpions executed an impeccable classic military parade in front of their eyes.

Before it was finished, Karl put his faded bluish eyes on Tobias and asked, "So, Tobias, tell me what's on your mind."
"I wanted to ask you a favour." There was a hint of nervousness in his voice.
"Ok, spit it out like the lizard you are."

Karl put his hands and fingers down to the scorpions to let them play and crawl onto him. "I want out, I mean, not being on the run anymore, but really out. You know, on the police side of the world; fuckers like snitches they get new lives under the protection of the government. Why don't we offer that? I could give you some of your enemies on a plate for a new identity and a place with a new start." There was silence in the room, except for the scorpion hissing noises filling the air.

Faster than Tobias spotted, Karl rose up and shook his right thumb against Tobias' Adam's apple, with a scorpion getting dangerously close. "I am the boss here for the reason that I perceive things. I know everything, and what you are saying now is utter rubbish. Have you any idea what would happen to the only honourable side of the law: ours? We would become washed out, similar to doughnut-eating policemen; we would sell our mothers like Nazis, and it would be the end of crime. I suggest you leave this idea before it was even born."

The door to the little kingpin's office was broken up in such a hurry it made even the nine reptile friends shiver. Janus put his large, but muscular head inside. "Boss, the police are on the way. I mean hoards of them, trying to surround us."

Karl's grip on Tobias tightened. "Tell me, are you the snitch? And tell me honestly, otherwise my little friend here will feast on you."

Janus stared, baffled at them then and words flew out of his humongous head that surprised the audience. "Did he tell you the thing about how he is the boss and knows it all? Let me tell you something. Leadership in any system and organisation can only partially be explained by an organisational structure. The reason is, leadership and management always have multiple faces. The human race has in many years been deceived to think of it in all kinds of forms, but often in some kind of pyramid, when it is in fact an intermixed and interwoven mess of multiple, fluid organisational structures, some official, others of various degrees of disclosure, in this game a caring lady, surrounded in ranks seemingly controlled by men, has an ever-increasing importance."

The situation demanded a rapid response to the incoming threat; instead Karl and Tobias were too dumbfounded to do anything but listen to the rant.

Janus continued his out-of-place speech, words that had grown inside him as frustration built up by carefully understanding he was not meant to be the one to take over his boss's role. "Therefore also, good leadership or management is not a perfect rule, or even a straight rule between up and down, but it sits in various roles coordinating with known and hidden peers. For a good structure to be managed in a good way, you need a different kind of leadership and management, to spread and optimise the product of that system or structure. In other words you will have leaders who care mostly about the upper parts, others caring for what is below, some who can judge in between, but you will also need some who don't care about the structure but instead put his or her effort in other values. These last ones can include doctors, mothers, wives, therapists, dentists, masseuses, priests and even your cleaning ladies or the pizza delivery boys, and the last ones are also by far the most important ones for success. Now the police are here and I couldn't care less about this organisation anymore. I put my life's work into this, just to see you pass it over to this green newcomer and to failure." He raised his gun and pointed it at both of them. "Fuck you both." It was obvious that he planned to kill them both before the cops arrived at the scene.

Tobias, who once had killed a family with five kids in cold blood, could not take it anymore. This was not supposed to happen. He cried, hard and uncontrollably.

Clarice busted in behind Janus and into him with such a brute force that he lost his piece. With her .22 cal. Smith & Wesson threatening to steal life, she shouted, "Stop this fucking farce or I'll shoot."

Scorpions and guns! As if that would improve the situation.

"BANG!"

The head fell down for today's feast. Karl turned his head over and looked at Clarice with surprise. Before he muttered a word, she started. "I'm the snitch, I'm the undercover, I'm the fucking police. He's faithful to you guys. Now, get your hands above your heads and kneel!"

पूरस्वाप

After the police had rounded up the convicts and her mission was accomplished, she went over to the stretcher with Tobias, removed the cover and peered at his face. Feelings of relief washed over her. What she had gone through for the purpose of duty, for the line of justice, it was too much for any person to be the lover of a gangster. One that kills people for change, one that would go physical with her, leaving a constant trail of bruises, on places that didn't show when dressed.

The sickness she had felt every time he had stared at her, touched her and cuddled her was finally over, but so was her will to stay a cop. This was the last time. It was time to start a new life, far away from crime and law.

To be on top

"The only thing I want is to be the best."

It's not just the alpha male that desires to be on top; every single man has a deep built-in drive to be the best. This simple fact can cause quite a pain because not everybody can be superior. Fortuitously, there might be a way because there are many traits were man can be the number one.

Dear Helge,

I have wanted to tell you the truth about what happened this summer for some time, and eventually I have gathered my courage and time to write down this letter for you. I understand that you have been disappointed with me, but I hope you will accept the reason why it was important for me.

It was the second-half kick-off of the World Cup final, the ultimate game to prove who is the champion of the world. We represented the underdog, of course, the team nobody would have expected to make it all the way to the final. Pressured into hopelessness, there was no way we could win this time. The score showed 0–2 in our disfavour and the break only provided us fifteen minutes of accumulated frustration.

We had been in a similar situation for most of the championship, hence, we committed ourselves fully to pushing every human limit, not known to man, into the unknown, in a desperate attempt to beat our opponents.

The whistle blew for kick-off like a tiny steam train and the ball rolled into motion. I saw Jackson pick it up with his toe, flip it in the air and kick it above Dave, it landing a metre in front of Benjamins' foot, perfect for him to catch.

Why is it we tend to call football players by their last names, with no resemblance of a title? I find it rather rude that we name our idols in a similar fashion, which we usually talk about street trash.

Jackson's rectangular-shaped face had a grimness; he never ever smiled. His failing stubs of hair would stand in any direction, even in a lack of any wind. His jaw would coerce out a biting phase, to tell the world: "I don't care what you think; I am in it only for the game."

Dave, my fellow forwarder, had a much nicer façade, a slightly plump face and body. He did not resemble a top-level athlete, but rather a guy relaxing on the couch, eating pizza and watching soft porn. He loathed his curly hair, but never found a solution to fix it. I envied Dave; he was a great shot, his upper legs were made of steel, or so we used to joke. How it came to be seemed a paradox and a riddle.

Benjamins was even more of a mystery for me; this dark, tall figure reminded me of an evil elf from a fantasy tale, for example *The Lord of the Rings*. When he moved on the football field, it almost seemed as if his feet didn't touch the ground. When Benjamins came towards the wrong goal, our goal, it reinvented everybody's belief in magic.

How to believe that we might win against such sorcery?

Benjamins' blurry feet surrounded the ball. I went straight towards him, boldly, even though I hated to go head to head with him. Don't misunderstand me: I was pretty fast with my feet as well, but could never match a legend like Benjamins. I tried to read his feint, but instead I ended up with a foot with a body attached sliding hopelessly in the wrong direction.

Benjamins continued his bewitched walk, with little hassle, all the way to the brim of the sixteen-metre mark before he lobbed it elegantly above John.

John was the sturdiest man I knew: tall, hard as a rock and always trustworthy. It was difficult to pass John; still, at that moment, it seemed easy like Sunday morning pancakes.

And there he stood, the legend himself, the best football player in the world: Shelter, the name that every young boy wanted on the back of his shirt. Golden skin, athletic, dark short hair and an easily recognisable grin always plastered on his face.

He hurtled around and hit the ball with a bicycle kick, gracefully shooting the ball with a twist towards the right corner. Arnie tried his best to jump towards it, but too late. The ball had entered the goal, what a goal! 0–3. We stood no chance.

Arnie had been our best player in this tournament; without his clever saves, his forethought on where to stand and block the ball, we wouldn't even have made it through the group play. I belive he had a sixth sense, homed on the future location of the ball. He was thinner than most football players and one could easily wrongly assume that he was malnourished.

Every drop of sweat, every little ache, drowned us in tiredness. But we had to bite our teeth harder together. We perceived this to be the only chance we had at the title, one we had stolen from under the competitors' feet. We needed to keep it going.

Being at such high altitudes left the air thin; every breath we took became its own stamina trial. Huffing and puffing, each and every one of us, as a big, bad wolf.

It felt like the very grass we ran on participated in the World Sweat Olympics.

Somehow we managed to get two goals before we hit eighty minutes; still we sensed no hope, we knew that even if we got a draw, it would kill us. None of us had any stamina left for extra rounds, let alone the inequitable penalties.

In the 88th minute, I managed in some strange way to perform a half-dirty tackle, without the referee blowing, and get the ball from Benjamins. Who would have thought? I crawled, lost on all fours, but Harald managed to pick it up and ran along to meet Develer, one against one.

If Develer had been a forwarder, he would have been famous; he would be the single player that might outperform Shelter in his own game. But fate, with plenty of partners, had decided he would become the best defender in the world.

Harald realised he would lose; just before impact he passed the ball back to me. A good move. I gained speed and did a one-touch kick, leaving it in a nice curve just in front of Dave. Dave picked it up with his left heel, flowing it to his front right and kicked it, unbelievably straight, at Diggins.

Diggins was short, in my view too much of a dwarf to be a goalie. What he did not own in length he could compensate with speed and agility. A pinch of half blond hair and grey eyes that looked as if they had cried all the blue out of them. He had teeth spread in every direction. Did he not have enough money for a tooth job?
He made a mistake; instead of standing and waiting for the ball, he made a pre-guessed jump to the right. We had 3–3.

The crowd went wild. We went wild. It was crazy, about to close as a draw. The referee signalled that he would add three minutes to the match.

Could we pull it through? Probably not, but we had to try.

The story of David and Goliath was such a cliché; the real world is different, and in it only two things exist: the winners and the losers. We all have experienced what happens to losers.

Both teams did last-minute swaps; our manager wanted me out, but I refused, convinced him I was still game, and he let me. Dave lost instead. Had I been a better person I would have loathed myself for stealing Dave's place.

Unlike the other players I had no special strength that identified me as a player. I was nothing but an overall performer; nobody really fancies average performers as they find them boring. I guess the real reason I commonly got to play forward with the team is that I had a gift of passing Dave the ball right where he needed it to get a goal.

This time I would be alone, against the clock, against the best. What had I done? Sabotaged the chances for the team? Put my own silly desires first? I did not know, did not put effort into elaborating about it. I consisted of 80 kilos of pure adrenalised exhaustion; emotion gone nuts.

The crowd had become ecstatic and wild, standing on both sides and screaming, singing and shouting. We failed to get the ball, just able to avoid a few attacks at our goal. The match was running short, with less than one minute left, John managed to snatch the token of the game, the ball, in his possession, giving it a hard kick the entire way to Terry.

Terry – fresh from the bench, the freckled wonder, who always had to sit on the bench. I believe he was better than me, but my synergy with Dave forced him ordinarily to suffer the bench or optionally to enjoy infamy in the field in the odd B-game.

He had more freckles than anybody else I knew; maybe he might be the world's freckle master. If he ever became a porn star, he would be a natural camouflage ninja.

I saw an opening in the defence, and I raced to be in position for the ball and gave a loud scream to signal that I was free. Terry, possibly rightfully, ignored me and opposed the defence himself. Develer was there, similar to a Chinese wall with a pillow. Terry went down and the ball was lost. Seconds were lost.

Only a few seconds left before the whistle blow.

But wait a minute. Terry got up faster than a blur and came on Develer from behind just before he could pass the ball along. What a determination. Filled with fresh endurance, he snapped the ball back and tunnelled through Develer's feet; it looked funny, the whole stadium laughed.

Before the laughter had settled, before most people realised what had happened, Terry had given the ball a nice upward slope with a twist, a curve that ended up close to where I stood, still unmarked. Diggins jumped towards it with his right hand, a white glove trying to catch it. I jumped up, head first, into the ball, white glove in my face, ball inside the goal, whistle went off, the crowd went haywire – no one was better than us.

We were the champions of the world!

The feeling encompassed me like multi-coloured foam, where each bubble erupted and exploded. The delight of knowing I was the best in the world was worth it all.

And then I lost control, exhaustion got the better of me and I missed my step, fell, everything became dark, faded. Disorientated on the ground, my consciousness wandered.

I woke up, just myself, an ordinary loser, paralysed from the waist down. I could never be the greatest in the world. But I was still a boy, with the deep urging need inside me to be the best.

Disappointment became me; my dreams were my own personal traitor. I looked out through my small windows. Outside were dark clouds bringing down bulks of heavy rain. Lightning ripped through the sky, scintillating a silver streak.

It alone inspired me to get up, with the usual preparation needed before I sat myself sturdily before the TV-set and started playing *EA Sports 2014 World Cup*.

I replaced some of the player names in my team from my classmates.

Dave, my fellow member of crime – not a real crime, of course, but the small devious things we are obliged to at my age. As were John, Harald, Arnie and Terry. I even named a player after you; mind you, he did not perform too well.

In the opposing teams I occasionally replaced the names with the last names of teachers and other adults.

After weeks and weeks, even months of playing, training, practice, I won the World Cup with a team against Diggins, Benjamins, Develer, Shelter and Jackson.

Finally, I was the best in the world, and there was no end of delight I felt in my wobbly legs! And that, Helge, is why I never came out to play with you this summer.

The wealth of stories we tell

"We might sometimes believe that our lives are boring and grey, but fear not, each of us has a story to tell."

He was lying there, relaxed, unconditionally, surrounded by the stale environment of uninteresting shades of white, tubes, coils, wires and the boredom of regularity. The slight odour of sick humans mixed with regular bacterial killers filled her nose. Her heart was flooded by feelings she wanted to share with him, but could not.

Precisely on 3/5/1954 at 04:15 was the moment when Gani, at the time a nameless boy, left the cosy world within the womb and peered out at a new world. A world that took little interest in him at first – after all he was simply another baby, among so many, too many. Even his parents, although happy, did not consider Gani to be much more than a baby.

The situation improved minimally during Gani's early years, but as he grew, he slowly commenced living a rather extraordinary life. In those days when people still did not wear devices to document every single, fleeting moment, it seemed that this eventful life, his adventures, would become but lost for us.

पूरस्वाप

"But he is a human, he is my brother; we can't just kill him like that." It was the same argument she always ended up with.
"But he is already as good as dead. He is nothing but a vegetable; he's been in a coma for three years, and is likely to stay there for the rest of his *life*," he replied with blatant anger.
"You don't know that, he could wake up anytime and come back to us," she countered.
"Ha, you're such a dreamer, even you don't really believe that." He punctured the sentence as if to signal that this was the last thing he wanted to say about it.
"No, but I hope he will. I hope so much," she cried.

Esther dissolved into tears. Dean was still a passionate being and put his arms around her to comfort her. Even though he was quite sure that stopping the life support for Gani would be the best for them. Not to mention the medical expenditure of keeping it running. Had he known any new argument for continuing the discussion, he would. He simply considered it to be somewhat gruesome to keep a person in a coma on life support for the purpose of making some other conscious living person feel good. He thought it to be a terrible state for Gani.

Esther, on the other hand, found difficulty in accepting the idea of having to "kill" her brother. She wanted nothing more than a miraculous solution to the problem. In such matters, hope and belief blended.

Dean loved Esther unreservedly. There were basically as few as two things that irritated him, and he found that unusual in a relationship. Most of his male friends had wives with whom they seemed to have no end of quarrels, most of them seemingly petty.

Esther broke out of their ring and went to the fridge to get half a litre of Coke, which she swallowed straight from the bottle. The two pedestals of irritation intermingled: her addiction to Coke and her affection for her brother.

Gani had never been around for anybody. He had simply disappeared, travelled around the world, living out a fantasy, and any time when he got in trouble, he became a family problem, or more precisely an Esther problem.

Even though Dean acknowledged that sometimes you have to accept other people's weaknesses in a relationship, he never let the chance fly by, day by day, week by week and by the by, to complain about the brother, in an endearing attempt to get her to welcome the idea of pulling the plug.

Halfway through the Coke, the alarming sound of their newly installed telephone rang loud enough for Esther to lose grip of the bottle, the black liquid pouring all over her, the floor and a few drops even found their way towards Dean.

"I don't mean to be Dean the Mean, but you'll need to clean this up while I pick up the phone." Dean grunted and turned to stop the noise.

"Hello. My name is Dr Lars Herrester Whyle of Umbridge Research Hospital, I am calling for Mrs Esther Krueger." The voice was overly formal and correct.
"That would be Esther DeHarm to you. I will go and get her. One moment."

Dean went over to Esther, quietly making gestures that she needed to take the call, while he would clean up the remaining mess.

She lifted up the receiver and announced herself.

The voice crackled on. "Dear Esther, so nice to speak with you. My name is Dr Lars Herrester Whyle of Umbridge Research Hospital. You might not have heard of me, but I have heard about you, or should I rather say about your brother."

"My, oh, my, there is not much I can help you with there. Are you aware of his situation?" She barely kept her voice together.

"Of course I am, dear, and I wanted to ask you for permission to help you with it. Let me explain, I am leading an effort to try to establish contact with those situations, those lost souls swimming in an ocean consisting of the medical state of a coma, where nobody seems to know anymore whether the best thing is to keep them alive or remove them to a different kind of peace."

Suddenly, he had her full attention; she just hoped this was not some kind of jest, but something true, like the miracle she had fantasised about.

He continued. "I have founded a research project where we use electroencephalograph, in other words electromagnetic monitoring of your brain waves as a tool to communicate with those who have no other way to communicate, such as your brother."

"Darn!" shouted Dean, fighting the flow of sticky, black fluid.

पूरसूवाप

That night, Dean had trouble sleeping. It was his speculations that haunted him. Thoughts about time, he had been dreaming of a time, with only him and Esther, without Gani, without – ah, to hell with it, he had to be honest with himself – without competition.

Did that make him a bad person? Probably, but Gani had never provided anything good to the family, ever. He was the adventurous brother who only made contact when he needed something, possibly an emergency fund of money or a good word to assist in solving some sticky problem with the world's bureaucracy.

But still, he did not desire to be a human like that, a bad person. With this new medical procedure, he could become stuck with Esther prioritising Gani for years to come. On the other hand, it could turn out negative, or for him positive, the scientific verification confirming the direction of pulling the plug.

He was not happy with himself contemplating these reflections. He stood up and went over to the bathroom, where his mirror image peered out at him suspiciously, to ask him, *What did you let the strain of the wicked mechanism of time turn you into?*

पूरस्वाप

She woke up, alone in bed, which was unusual. She felt strangely awake and with a fleeting sense of energy building within. *Happiness.* Without dressing, she left their bed and went silently downstairs to the workstation in Dean's home office. She needed to do some research.

The procedure was still in its infancy and there were those who opposed it and called it "hocus pocus" – nothing but a magic trick; she clearly saw that this was not the case. The results spoke for themselves: approximately forty-seven percent of the subjects showed awareness and communication skills. Initially, it was performed with the help of MRI, but as MRI was both expensive and cumbersome, the team, with Dr Herrester Whyle in the lead, had developed a method to use something as readily available as EEG. The secret to monitoring responses was to ask the patient to picture himself or herself playing tennis as "Yes". For a negative response they used the imagination of the subject running as fast as possible. These imagined activities would leave clear responses on the EEG and in turn it opened an approach to communicate, where previously there had been none, provided they still had some cognitive processes intact. Behind the cards it would seem obvious that this method was to become the future standard.

What if Gani did not react? What would she do? Dean would for sure insist to give him rest. But Esther did not want to; she imagined that she sensed life in him. Gani had to answer them. It had to be this way.

पूरस्वाप

"Nothing."

The music of Coldplay's 'Clocks' was playing softly over the PA. *The lights go out and I can't be saved.* In the room were the great doctor, his assistant Mr Thomas Tree, Esther, Esther's nurse friend Lina, Dean and of course Gani. It had been really nice of Lina to show up, to show native support from someone who understood the environment from the inside. They had tried for two hours to reach through to Gani, to no avail. Despair was seeping into Esther.

Why did they play music on the PA anyway? After all this was a hospital. *Oh I beg, I beg and plead, singing.*

Again Dean held her, and she let him, crying. She knew well what it signified: it meant death. Death was too much for her to handle. "I am so sorry, Mrs DeHarm," said the now intrusive voice of the doctor.

"Wait."

Come out of things unsaid.

As much as science can do for us, help us with, it still cannot create miracle cures – bring back someone who has gone beyond the barrier of a long-lost reef.

It seemed hopeless for her; comparable to being somewhere abandoned on the seven seas, without oars, without sail, without a float – just her, alone, drowning.

"Wait," Lina cried out. "Look here."

As synchronised clockwork they all turned to her, moved in closer and looked at her finger pointing excitedly at the EEG readout.

She continued. "If you study really closely, like the miniature writing on a contract, you can see patterns."
The doctor quickly grabbed the paper, scrutinised it and said, "Let me see. Hmm. You are quite correct: it is there, just very vague."
The doctor turned to Thomas; his eyes were furious, almost red, but his voice was still remarkably controlled. "Thomas. Care to explain?"
Thomas caught the evil eyes upon him. "Sir, it must have been the calibration."
The doctor turned around again, in pure disrespect. "Make sure you calibrate it properly now, hastily, so we can continue."

Am I a part of the cure?

What a change, the room had been turned from failure, from sadness into an explosion of pure joy. Even Dean got caught up in it; it had been unbelievable, to be there, participating in the forefront of science, to be one of the first breaking the barrier to something new.

Maybe it would not be that bad after all?

They got to ask questions, in turn, and Gani answered them with yes and no to the best of his ability. This way they found out that he was not suffering, but it was sort of boring being in his state and he found happiness in communicating with them.

Lunch hour crept upon them as a sneaky weasel. Nobody wanted to go, but eventually nature took its course and they left, simply to return about an hour later.

Thomas ripped off the EEG reading from lunch and showed it to the doctor. "What do you think this means?"
The doctor hadn't forgotten the earlier incident and wasn't interested. "What?"
Thomas was persistent. "Well, if you glance over here, during lunch the patient continued to make the patterns of yes and no, repeatedly even if nobody was present in the room. What do you make of it?"
The doctor studied it closer. "Strange, this makes little sense. Why would he make responses without us asking questions? It's not like he can tell us anything interesting with simple yes and no responses."

Dean snatched the paper out of the doctor's hands. The doctor became startled by the rudeness. "It's an SOS," said Dean.
The doctor nearly forgot himself and said something nasty, but stopped himself just in time. "SOS, a cry for help? But he told us that he was doing fine."

Dean looked at the doctor, not without pride for having taught such an important figure something. "It's Morse code, as we have showed Gani a way to communicate with us, he is now showing us how to improve it. With Morse code, it's enough with two responses, in this case, yes means a dot and no means a dash, by putting them in sequence Gani can essentially tell us anything, with proper language."

While the doctor and Thomas understood, Lina and Esther had never learned Morse code and looked at Dean with strange, shining eyes.

Dean answered the stare. "It means that we can talk to him and he can talk to us, unrestrained. There is no end to the possibilities." Wow! It seemed like happiness would never end.

Home, home where I wanted to go.

Through the method of Morse code, Gani Krueger was able to communicate several compendiums of wacky stories and adventures. And what marvellous tales they were.

The Cure

*"Good and Evil co-exist in a symbiotic
relationship of constant conflict."*

**Ten thousand years ago the world was not as unforgiving
as today; it was virtuous. Innocence has a tendency to allow
for aspiration, and later transpiration of great evil. This
gave rise to Embarico, post-mortem named the Devastator,
the most gruesome being ever to set his dirty two feet on
this planet.**

Already in his late youth Embarico rose through the ranks and
abolished any resistance against him. He didn't believe in any
honour or duty, only his own law, to rule and enslave. By the age of
thirty-three, he had risen to be the de-facto ruler of the globe.

A rule constituted of any horror possibly imaginable but worse.
Slaves, rape, murder, slaughter, death games, treason, burning,
torture, fear and agony became obligatory parts of an ordinary
day. No act seemed horrible enough or malicious enough to clench
Embarico's thirst for evil.

Embarico's only weakness was his love for the most dazzling girl in the world. As his main queen, Beatrice shone with such bewitchment that the sheer beauty would physically stun any man who laid his eyes upon her.

As his mate, Beatrice became the single person with access close enough to the Devastator to ever cause him harm. Which she did, treason done right. Rescuing the world from its greatest Evil, with a promise for it never to happen again.

That accomplishment became the birth of the modern ages, the rebuilding of our space-floating orb, a chance to become a new and mature world.

Indeed, during the years there have been plenty of Embarico's descendants, legal, pure and bastards hiding their true identities to escape the shame of their ancestor.

An organisation rose, with the fitting name "the Cure", founded with the sole purpose to hunt down and brutally annihilate Embarico's descendants and wipe them forever off the surface.

As civilisations progressed, grew and fell, the Cure hunted and terminated, with great cost to its own members, every known bloodline of Embarico to this day.

Today there is only one left, King Bario, who has escaped the modern world into the far-away mountains where Castle Everbore can be found.

Luckily, the organisation known as the Cure, although strained and depleted, still consisted of one strenuously strong man.

Kedrian the avenger travelled towards Everbore as a part of his quest. It could possibly have been the most remote castle on the globe; to get there he had to fight against giant scorpions, hordes of snakes, the dark elves of old and a good number of King Bario's elite soldiers.

He had to traverse various devious traps and hindrances, and he on two occasions became captured, just to use his wit, or lack of such, to escape, with helpful assistance of pure strength. It was not an adventure that any normal man or pack of such would survive.
In the end, when he arrived at the castle, he wasn't even half the man as when he had started. What he had brought with him on the way was a bag of experience he would rather be without. Nevertheless, he was finally close to the ultimate goal, not only his own, but representing every living species' goal: to prevent the world from the possibility that any seed of the Devastator could ever return to rise again.

The castle seemed mysteriously abandoned. Kedrian was exhausted, not purely in body but also in mind; he did not even notice that something was wrong within the pressing silence. He entered the main entrance and waltzed through.

Spider webs? Empty halls? No resistance? Chambers and hallways filled with a gloomy silence built the feeling of an unwelcome presence. The fumes floating through his nostrils contained a bitter aftersmell of mould.

His thoughts lingered only on creating death, the one eradication that mattered. He discovered the location to be strangely abandoned. Had he arrived too late? A slimy, hard choke of fear pulsed his Adam's apple tightly. Had King Bario managed to stall him long enough to escape? It was, however, not surprising with the slow progress he had made.

That bastard Bario, he deserved to feel the raw steel splitting him out of existence. Kedrian started running, breaking the timeless interwoven pieces of cobweb, making haste to the throne room.

Arriving at his destination, he saw the king sitting on a chair beside a table of chess. Waiting patiently for him. "Would you care for a game of chess?"

Kedrian had no mood for games; he owned a one-track mind. "Not at all, I am here to end you." Kedrian lifted his sword and prepared for attack, but got interrupted.
The king made a sweeping motion and said, "It is only fair that you let a dying man have a last wish. What I wish is for us to play a game of chess. If you win you can kill me in any way you wish, but in the unfortunate case that I would win—"
Kedrian cut him short. "I will grant you your life?"
"Of course not. You will still be able to kill me. The difference is that I am humbly given the gift of joy of winning the game first."

Kedrian agreed, not that he cared much for games; actually he was bred for one purpose and cared for little except his mission, and it was this realisation that convinced him. The fact that his sole purpose in life would soon be over, it scared him more than any opponent or obstacle; he wanted to savour this moment for a long time.

Somewhat unfairly, the king started with the white pieces. "So tell me, traveller, what do you think you will accomplish by murdering me?"

Kedrian waited in silence for a while before he answered. "You are the last descendant of Embarico, the most terrible creature to ever wander on these lands. The world cannot truly be at peace with this terror until every last one of Embarico's children are forever removed from the ranks of the living."

The game of chess was a difficult one; they both had years of training in the art, and such was it that this could turn out to become a long evening. Kedrian noticed that the king appeared to be seventy years old, even though in reality he was only thirty-five. What toll had life had on this king?

"That's so many years ago. Just because an ancient father of mine was gruesome does not mean that I, or any of my children, if I would ever be permitted to have some, would have any resemblance to Embarico. No, my little one, I think you are on a witch hunt without a real purpose, led by some of the very characteristics that you want to rid the world of: fear and hate."

The words made Kedrian uncomfortable; in fact, the king repulsed him. He found no savour; this was the king trying cheap tricks to manipulate him. He would not allow it; he rose up and roared out, "There is nothing you can do to prevent my redemption!" His chair fell with a thump.

In the moment Kedrian swung his sword for the final kill, the king blew a till now hidden dart, hitting Kedrian's neck. Likewise, the king's head was chopped off and fell down to share company with the fallen chair. Kedrian fell back in surprise, losing his sword and using both hands to remove the dart. He sensed the scent it emitted.

He was familiar with the odour – a poisonous dart, but not the quick kind. It would take him maybe a month of suffering before he died unless he could muster an antidote. He gathered head and sword and started the long journey back home.

Behind the king's main chamber was a secret passage with a peering-hole. There stood the king's unknown twin brother laughing his heart out. Even though the price had been the highest kind, he was now forever liberated.

The strife for water

"Some boys are of the opinion that water is purely for topical use, like there is no water in soda."

Everybody wants something, everybody needs something, but often it is a created craving, fictitious to display a very individual point. Similar to a knife cutting butter, such desires will all fall to a human's primary need. It was the intense feeling of dryness, sandpaper, the desert tongue rubbing in his mouth. Dehydration deluxe; he needed water, right now!

Around seven to eight years old is the age a child starts to convene the picture of its parents as gods, a kind of symbolic moon and sun. (The beginning of this process starts at an earlier stage.) It will last about four to five years until such a belief is usually torn to pieces by the hard realism of existence. In that time they will be able to suck into themselves a barren copy of the good and bad sides of their deities. To some degree they even become "Mini-Me"s, mirrors, reflections of their masters.

When they realise that the parents are in fact no more than another bunch of human beings, suddenly they wish to fight against human weakness, which now, to some degree, can be called their own.

The fight against their parents' bad habits, at the same time as these habits are growing as phantoms within themselves, is vicious and in most cases bound to fail. Somewhere in their twenties, they will probably resign and give up, and you will hear them say, "I didn't realise it till now, but I have become so much like my father/mother."

Let me offer some hope in such a depressing ring, at least two ways to prevent this pattern from continuing: one is that the kid actually manages to break loose, or the better option is that you as a parent understand the mechanisms of this paradox, and work out your own issues before and during the young years of your kids, and take the rap for them.

How did it all start? Not by his choice. It had never been his idea. He did not even get a say. His mother had decided that they should take a trip to Trondheim. Seven hours driving non-stop. No breaks except to urinate; he prevalently needed to pee.

None of the sweet, caramelised liquorish candy that he relished – his father would always bring them on their driving trips, even short trips – were offered. He did not desire to drive any lengthy trips, trips made him dizzy. Nauseous. He needed to sit in the front, see the road. But his mother would not let him, complained that it was not safe for him, as he was nothing more than a little kid.

Darn, he had already become eight years old, he knew plenty of bad words, and he could beat up most of his classmates. But no, his mother would not permit him to sit in the front seat, even when she knew he would get car-sick. Puke all over. He would suffer queasiness for an extended period before he could relieve himself – a terrible wait in agony.

What was it with Trondheim anyway? He wanted to stay at home and play the new Giana Sisters game, bring some of his mates over. They wouldn't dare say no. Nothing but game on the whole night long. His mother was against video games; luckily, she fell asleep first and then their house became a free port for pleasures. It was lucky that he had developed a sense of creativity to cause much harm.

What entertainment could a car possibly offer? Reading the latest issue of Donald Duck was out of the question; he could not sit in the front and watch the traffic, and she did not let him play on his harmonica. Was she out of her mind? No candy? He needed candy, he needed distractions, and he needed them now. Music? No, she had forgotten his tunes; boring, ugly melodies sounding out of the speakers, idiotic adult sounds on the radio.

What was wrong with adults? Did they not own any rationality?
Of course he had to remind his mama continuously on the way how stupid she was, and elaborate on his needs, again and again and again. Then he would play his harmonica. He tried to perform the theme of 'Nattønske' by Sigmund Groven, but in reality a set of random sounds emerged. It came to such an accumulation of irritation that his mother furiously stopped the car, threw him out of the vehicle and disappeared.

He wondered if a mother was allowed to just leave her son alone, behind on a European route. What should he do now? Walk along the road? There were no computer games here, nothing to do. It was even more boring than inside the car. Did his mama not realise that this was even worse?

At least he got fresh air and his head felt well, even though the freshness became easily penalised by fear, the creeping anxiety of being alone and not understanding what to do. Would his mother return? Would he have to stay alone all night? Would gruesome monsters, like snakes – big ones – come and eat him?

He tagged along the lane. There wasn't much traffic, and he spent most of his time alone with the road for company. Maybe it was possible to walk the entire way to Trondheim?

Further down the lane he discovered a junction, a small trail cascading into parallel railroad tracks. He found a rusty nail among the stones and placed it, without further ceremony, on the railroad tracks. He quickly left the tracks and waited.

He played the harmonica; Sigmund Groven would have cried in pain.

Fun and joy. The wait lasted no more than ten minutes, seemingly less, before the train came through. The train did not even flinch; it cared not about the obstacle he had put in its path. Picking it up, what once was a nail had become flat and alluring. Fascinating in an odd and peculiar way, a malformed shape, as nature had chosen it to be.

He searched, with great excitement, for more metal, but in vain. Again he hit the road, trailing further on. That's when it hit him: first, the thirst; secondly, the hunger. He direly needed food and water. How could his mother leave him here to suffer? Did she not care?

He could not even play the harmonica anymore, too dry to even try, like the air would suck itself inwards instead of blowing out his strange mishap of a tune.

He promenaded, increasing his speed in uncoordinated increments. After a while his mouth dried up. He paced to something of a snail. He wondered if his mother would forgive him for being a menace. Would it be enough for him to say he was sorry, for her to give him food?

Hydration had to come first.

A white, medium-sized vehicle stopped close to him. The right window wound down and a man's face appeared against the fading day. Three days of beard and concern addressed him. "Hey, kid, where are you heading?"

He told the truth, simple as he was. After a few more questions, he had explained everything. No longer outside, but in the back of the car. White on the inside, similar to the outside. The driver's clothes bore the same shine. He could be a chameleon and disappear, be one with everything. Be white, swift and invisible.

But hydration first; even chameleons need to drink.

The ingratiated stranger took him to a roadside diner and bought them some food. He got a big, shiny bottle of Voss water, exclusively for him. Today's small miracle, almost unbelievable.

Greedy and needy, he choked himself on the bottleneck while water poured down on him and into him. Refreshing him in a new and different way, it was beautiful. It seemed like paradise. Even though he knew it would last only as long as the bottle did not become empty, if it ever would.

The man laughed at him and said, "Now, let's see if we can get you to your mum."

Saving the world

"She is hiding something."

The Animal drummed his stick, merely drops hit the low-quality building with irritation and eagerness. Sticky, humid and a tad too chilly air filled the room. It was always like this: shitty, gritty and unbearable. Still I somehow endured, one day at a time. It was my home, at least for now.

It wasn't the contents of the message that disturbed me. I suffered uncontrollable shakes; that could be excused by the bitter weather. It was the fact that I had perceived the message at this moment.

"You are refusing to admit the truth," she tried to provoke me.
"Don't make it all look bleak. We both have rather good occupations; get by and survive," I countered. I didn't desire her to win this argument.

She lifted her left hand and formed a quote. "The problem has always been that you are weak; you do not want to see the reality. You hide yourself conveniently in a private pool of fear."

She knew how to upset me; she repeatedly did.

We were psychics, more often referred to as "freaks" – people born with certain psychic or loosely related skills. We had no power to choose the skills ourselves; it just dawned on us somewhere between the age of three and seven. In most cases, we got useless skills, but sometimes they indeed had some value.

We both worked as specially hired consultants – nice wording to hide a crude schema of fortnight contracting for the police.

I wanted the discussion to move in a different direction. "You are wrong. This world is not comparable to the movies. How many times have we seen the inspector or detective who tries to understand the psychopath to catch him? It's stupid, you can't possibly get under the skin and comprehend the psychopath without being one yourself. We know better, the police hire psychics like us because they are not capable of finding the clues themselves. By doing so we make the difference."

She would not let me stop her. "Do we? Really? Any advantage we give the police, the criminals can counter. What makes you believe there are no freaks supporting the other side? You flip a coin; both sides are eventually the same. We don't make the difference, we just fill the role of expendables in an arms race."

I saw her biting her lips; somehow the humidity always caused her skin to crawl, too dry, specially her lips. It resembled an old conversation, a re-run, a black and white movie, similar to all of our conversations. We used to date, far back in the grey mass of memory. Back then I did not understand how to control my ability; even though I do not regret it anymore, it became the ruin of us.

I knew very well what she was hiding, nothing new. But I did not understand why I wasn't able to suppress my ability on her. It baffled me. Was I starting to turn old, sour and incapable?

I deeply desired to win our conversation, even though it never would return any pleasure. "Elise, you have to have faith in the world. Psychics are usually more developed people and therefore have higher standards, which in turn guide us to become a more righteous species. We choose to be on the good side of life. Take this new case I am working on: the serial killer cuts their victim in a total rage. The result is an odd number of body parts shattered in every direction. I have never in my time witnessed anything as disgusting. No psychic would ever be capable of such manslaughter. On the contrary, we will be the pivotal piece in catching the culprit."

Elise's ability was to store large quantities of information in her brain and somehow put two and two, or even thousand and thousand, together and discover the context and inconsistencies – an invaluable skill in cross-examinations and scrutinising case material. Most of her time was spent either auditing cases or reading up on the events that turn this globe around.

No wonder she had a quirk for losing faith in the wonders of the world.

पूरस्वाप

I reached into my pockets and searched around. I handed her a lip balm with fresh-flower scent. The same one I always gave her. She consistently forgot them and was as happy as always to borrow mine. I left her busy with it, almost as a rehearsed play.

My home, in some mysterious way, pretty much replicated the miserable outdoor life. I fell flat down on the couch to relax.

In the summer, Trias did not exist; just desolate sand, resembling a hostile desert. People lived elsewhere, where existence was good, sometimes on the edge of romantic. In the winter, the climate changed drastically, to such a degree that even if its location was dreadful, it was the lesser evil in close to a 1000 kilometres.

Trias was a temporary urban establishment, built up in a short two weeks consisting of whatever provisory material could be gathered. At its peak it would house up to fifty-five million people. It was the pinnacle of organic city engineering. Even the most trained eyes had problems spotting the end of it.

It was a Mecca for all sorts of business, including speculative crime. And the gods kept heaving raindrops at my feeble roof. It was not a real home. I always wanted to be someone important, a person leaving a dent in the world, a teacher of young kids, to inspire them to become better citizens. Once declared a psychic, mechanisms were put in place to prevent you from becoming anyone important. Normal people were afraid of us, put in place numerous measures to stop us from "taking over".

Once more the unspeakable has transpired.

If it ever could be called stillness, the phone broke it. "He has done it again, I need you to get here at once."

Justin: my handler, my primary police contact and the officer in charge to find our perpetrator – his voice pushed up against my ear. I jumped to my feet; finally, time to get down to business.

I favoured Justin as my handler; we'd developed mutual respect, which provided me with advantages above most contracted psychics, who often were left to suffer various degrees of humiliation.

Less than half an hour later I met Justin. We mimicked two lost souls, swimming in mud and rain. I handed him a scorching cup of coffee. The disposable kind, which would struggle to maintain its structure for the same amount of time it took to finish it. I found it strange that the liquid on the outside should be such a destructive force in comparison with the dark liquid on the inside.

Justin reeled off facts, the status in his usual, de-facto manner. Oh, how I loved this: the thrill, the unmistakable stench of being close, putting the pieces together to get a solution. A positive and exciting feeling possessed me. Today, Trias would become a safer place.

The smell of not so fresh coffee beans hitting our nostrils provided vitality in this dump, a short moment of euphoria.

I didn't even get time to have a look at the gruesome scene, the display of something that once had been a human, disgraced, mortified, cut to a thousand pieces and spread around in perfect chaos.

The murderer is near.

Immediately, I stopped paying attention to Justin and started to scan the area. He didn't notice and continued talking to me even as I examined the outskirts of the crime scene. I swept the periphery for clues, and was lucky: I noticed a silhouette a couple of blocks below.

As soon as I spotted him, I ran.

I broke all protocols. Chasing is not something a psychic is supposed to do. That's to be left to the professionals, the real police. Following the person in front of me was an extremely stupid thing to do. My health was made for dozing on sofas, drinking beer and watching crap TV, not this high-performance stuff.

Luckily, the murderer could not have been much better off. As I huffed and puffed my way forwards, the distance was closing up, in my favour. Strangely, one would believe a highly dangerous criminal to be in better shape. The drums of the Animal had journeyed inside to my heart, thundering around my flesh.

Suddenly, the shadow in front of me disappeared.

Bugger, I had screwed it up. Broken procedure; tried to be the hero. The price would certainly be my job. A psychic without an occupation equalled an anchor without an ocean, usually falling through society.

Pushing myself round a corner, I found the guilty person again, climbing up the wall to the left of me. On the limb, there was not much choice other than to follow. My hands had become cold, stale, and did not want to grip the surface. Yet, I forced myself to continue; it was no longer a matter of making a difference. It was a matter of saving my own buttocks.

The hunted entered the building through an open window two storeys above me. It comforted me; even the pathetic indoor environment would be a welcome change.

When I finally got to the same window and jumped in, I was not prepared for either of the surprises.

The dull thud on the side of my head suggested a blunt instrument. Not enough to put me out of my misery, but enough to hurt. That would have been better than being face to face with Elise. What cruelty it is to stand in front of a person capable of performing such evil deeds and comprehend that you once loved this person.

I couldn't utter a word, but didn't have to as she started. "You see, we will never make a difference if we do not stand up for ourselves. We need to treat us, the psychics, as the superior race and deface the normal humans. Today we let them treat us like shit and dictate our miserable lives. And we let them; it's time to make a stand, make a change. Let them burn."

I could not fathom what my ears picked up; this was above crazy. "No, we cannot become monsters, commit to evil just because we've not been treated justly. We need to be better than that. To be the better part of the human race, we need to display maturity, justice, dignity and honour."

The words did not sound like me; I never usually either thought or said such eloquent words. What was happening to me?

The dim light of the small room we were stuck in flickered to outside the window. The sound of the traffic and of a thousand people, on their way from or to their own busy bubbles. But no outside influences would affect us now; we were lost in our own island with oceans separating us from the real world.

"You are wrong! If we stand still and don't fight for our rights, we will forever be the suppressed race. What I do might be radical, but we need to be radical; we need to join forces together and claim what is our right."

"By killing the innocent?"

"How can any person who participates in organised racism against a race be innocent? Do you conceive Justin to be different, just because he treats you well? Well, I got news for you: a slave-driver

105

is still a slave-driver even if he handles his slaves with respect. It is true that some of us manage to secure positions where existence is bearable. We survive, but are we happy? Do we even come close to our dreams? What about all the other freaks, those who don't pull the limited number of lucky straws in life? They have nothing; they are living lives on the street, in the gutter. They are not even freaks; they are bums. What happens when you no longer can perform your job? You will take rank among the nameless out in the dark."

Somehow, her elaborating made more and more sense, too much sense. I still tried to counter-argue. "There are efforts to help the ones lost out on the wagon—"

She would not let me finish. "Yes, pitiful efforts that provide a few of us with a free and pathetic meal or a used rag every now and then. You call that help? It is a part of what keeps us inferior. No, my friend, we need to claim the power. Join me; let's create an organised stand for our rights. Let's save the world."

Believe me, I wanted to let go of reality. Join her, maybe we could melt together again. Perhaps we could be the difference through her plan of pain. We embraced each other, not only with the eyes and arms, but kissing, desperate, lost, hidden from the dark nature surrounding us; we had rediscovered absent passion.

Unfortunately, everybody knows that it's utter madness to believe that a single person can save the world.

She loves you.

With tears running, dripping below, I dipped into my pockets. No lip balm this time, but a small and bleak steel knife. Still embraced, she could not detect my deeds; carefully, yet firmly, I sliced her neck, to her own death. Blood poured out faster and fiercer that the rain fell outside. The fresh odour of red reminded me of copper on current.

पूरस्वाप

My memories have vanished. Justin told me that I was still crying when he found me. He protected my deeds with lies.

We have to be content with changing ourselves; living our lives in a way that matters makes the difference. We have to rid the world of madness, cruelty and evil.

I knew, though, that my time as a crime fighter was over even though Justin would keep me. I could not keep myself; too many years I had let life rule me. Time cried "ripe" for a change, even though it would be done in small steps, the right steps.

She loved you.

Sweet pain

"We never felt closer than when we were apart."

Even though the brain encompasses a wonderful ability to filter out the boring, sad and even horrid moments of our lives, the faded memories will still not route the suffering of longing.

Does he remember? she thought.

A harmony echoed the ripples of her own contemplations. The silence of nature, the water and her breath reassured her, away from the desperate sense of loneliness.

She remembered too well their first time in bed. Sweaty pearls mixed with Arnica oil. In the process of massaging her whole body, he had finally arrived at her head. His fingers, meticulously searching for new knots to stimulate, found a bulge. Shocked, with a hint of tease, he looked at her.

"Mmm... you have an alien brain," he said, provocatively.
"What?" she responded, amazed.

It was such a surreal experience, a surprise. Where did he pull it from? As an immediate reaction she tilted her head backwards and laughed. Had there been a hint of hidden nervousness?

"Really, I can feel it here."

His fingers pricked, stroked and pushed the lump on the back of her head. It felt nice when he did, somewhat relaxing. She just wanted to descend into a restful state of peace.

"And how, might I say, does this prove that I am an alien?" she asked.

"Easy, aliens have abducted you and they have operated this device in the back of your brain. You might not even have known it, probably you have no recollection of it anymore. That would be quite realistic, indeed." He smiled with humour.

This time they both fell back and laughed off his ridiculousness. Such silliness was strange for her. She missed it with pain similar to a knife in an already open wound.

A squirrel scream brought her back to the tranquil present. Not too far away, up on a tree branch, the rodent chippered desperately. But why, what did it want? Even though the sound was intrusive, within the sophisticated filter of Mother Nature it grew into a part of the music of the wild. Music created in the soft spots between silences.

Does he still remember?

They met, as many do initially, in a dark corner of a nightclub. Lights changing colour and flashing, smoke infecting the air. Already at that time he was a ticking bomb of frivolous joy, with jokes, absurdities and fun. How could she not like him?

Later, they ended up at an after party with some of her friends. The opening kiss, then another one, the third, it would have continued if not for a rather irritating disruption. A second couple started quarrelling, breaking the spirit of the party. An atrocious mood flooded the place.

They went home to their respective households. Her heart pumped beats of fear; the same fear that filled her now. Would she ever see him again?

She could not go out the next few days. She was too occupied with work, with her own personal life, but when she decisively found time, he was waiting for her. Relief shuddered through her limbs comparable to a descending earthquake. Would he notice it?

Would it matter if he did?

They left the club and went for a stroll in the park. My, he could turn a promenade into a continuous journey of discovery. Everything he observed would be a potential toy for him, something to ridicule in any which way possible. Could it be that she was also a toy to him? The night ended with the climax of them entangled in each other's embrace, kissing, on the edge of the park with night birds as the only spectators. Again, they separated, with a promise: one of meeting again the next day.

With her eyes dwelling deep into his, the next day, over a simple chicken-based fast-food meal, she asked him, "What would you like to do tonight?"

He answered her, returning the same question. Silence. They ate more, and looked at each other with short, brief glimpses. It was more than looks, more than eyes; it was a glittering shimmer from the hidden deep below. How could she not fall for him?

"I know what you want."

Now, what was it with this squirrel? It didn't give up? The music of the forest and the water was faltering, turning into a loud screeching concert performed by this squirrel. Wait, there were two squirrels, fighting each other for a nut? Possibly they were performing the archaic rite of domination of an area. She was unsure; it was difficult to see the details from her location with darkness gradually creeping up on her.

Everything surrounding her was peaceful but yet foreign, disrupted by this strange competition of material property.

Won't he forget? she thought.

Back in bed, he would throw her around and continue.

"You know, many cats, they have a parasite called toxoplasmosis, which can affect their brains and their behaviour. This parasite can also select human hosts; in fact, estimates are that approximatly one-third of the earth's population is infected. In turn this parasite can influence what we do and how. It might sound much the same as an episode of Star Trek, but in reality, it is the remarkable truth," he said.

"Sure," she replied.

She didn't believe him one bit, but he knew how to prove himself. What is a bed without an iPad? The collective truth of Wikipedia right at your fingertips. Again she got hit by the hammer of astoundment.

"But that is not everything, the human body comprises 100 trillion bacteria, ten times more than it has cells, which live in various

degrees of harmony with the body, some of which can influence the choices we make in life. Each single person has their own unique microbiota signature. They can, for example, influence what kind of people we like, surround us with, and even choose as partners, based on what bacteria other people carry," he recited.

"So basically what you are insinuating is that our perception of free will is in fact us being played in some kind of puppet game of our numerous small masters?" she responded.

Again he laughed, and she followed suit.

It had been days as sweet as pine extract. It all had been so new to her. The way he seemed to care more for her than himself. Now she was here alone even if she was surrounded by life. She realised the answer. Of course he remembered, and always would.

She stared up into the vast sky, the stars greeting her. Every moment from the past, good and bad, lives on forever as light particles travelling through the cold universe. Pilgrims telling the tale of what once happened, again and again for billions of years, until they reach the very end fabric of the universe.

She used the question to hide the sweet pain behind the real questions. "Would he ever understand that she actually was an alien? That she was forced to leave him?"

The most important question of them all, the one that made her tears rain down, into the water as drops of despair, but maybe also hope, was, "Would she ever meet him again?"

The spy

"There is no honour among broken men."

The many tales of spies rarely reflect the tragedies of reality. Forced by various circumstances, be it greed, poverty, family or love, spies act in treasonous ways, often paying the ultimate price: loneliness and isolation.

"I suggest that you think of this not as a shakedown, but rather as an opportunity…"

The remaining words emerged garbled into his mind. It wasn't the sombre atmosphere in the living room: the mixed scent of fresh, new cigar fumes, with untimely layers of old and stale scent from just too many brown sticks. Nor was it the reedy feeling of their success: the hunters picking up their prize.

No, it was only him, being utterly annoyed with himself. He should have expected what was coming. He should have known better. Somehow tricking him to believe that self-loathing would be the solution.

It had started like it usually did, with him travelling – away from his sorry excuse of a *home* – for an extended period. Life never really started until he put his first, resolute step out of the door. In the beginning he had pondered, like a whirlpool filled with a dark cloud, about the reason why everything went totally wrong. Heck, he had even fought against it, tried to repair his marriage – but to no avail.

How can one mend something that had always been broken? What a failure he'd proven to be, once upon a time to jump, head first, into a fallen nest.

As long as it was possible to spend a lot of hours out of home, as much as work permitted him, as long as they had young kids together and a divorce would mean financial ruin – the inherent fear of loss of freedom and privileges – as well as giving him the opportunity to repeat all his mistakes again, he preferred to fake it. Or so he convinced himself, but the truth was, he'd be too much of a coward to break free, even if time would unearthly prove to him that the cost of this choice would be his ruin.

To his surprise, he excelled in the art of lying. The nice "I love you" phone calls every evening, back to the household, were only topped up with her nice replies, both caught in a marvellous game of con.

Once in the hotel, work never became a priority; he grasped too well that it was possible to get away with the least effort, better utilised like a lonesome hunter, to discover what he actually wanted: a woman to spend some moments with.

Often they found him, just like this time. Being unhappily married reeked its own magic. He attracted females comparable to Mr Superglue.

There was no division on status, education, nice or cruel, beautiful or normal. What did he care? It was a short-time ride. He thought of it as entertainment even though deep down he knew it as his struggle of survival.

This time around, she was quite nice and a bit too elegant for his taste – with posh and expensive habits. He couldn't handle being beaten at his own game.

Late and long dinners at expensive restaurants. Always the right wines and the correct dress. Evocative speech patterns and some awareness about everything.

He could quite enjoy it.

It was never meant to be this way. In his younger days, he'd been an actual dreamer and an idealist. Not exclusively in what love and family would bring him, but also in any matter of man – life had taught him a harsh lesson, knocked him down on the pavement. He had never gotten up again, but crawled along as a fungicide amoeba, as the complete opposite of his dreams.

Once in his lifetime he had written a piece, a piece of belief, a piece of understanding, a naïve essay on how the world turned around. He had spent a whole summer getting the letters in the correct order; among all and every thing that happened in this world it was the only thing he could remember, as if it was laser etched into his brain:

"The known question about state governance systems: 'Which one is better than the other? Communism, socialism, despotism, dictatorship, monarchy, commercialism, fascism, etc.' is that revolutions and government swaps have a tendency to lead to yet another power or system that has its own faults to prove. As a catch twenty-two, this leads to a perception of helplessness for all the people searching for a solution to crack this nut. Most fall into the trap of thinking that democracy seeded with a bit of commercialism is the only solution. Others tend to prefer some extreme fundamentalist direction.

As in the novel *1984* it leads to sides fighting each other, enemies for the reason of sustaining balance, where no one necessarily is the better.

Several politicians have had a grasp of the real solution, a kind of over-governing set of values, yet they often fail in the understanding of how high it needs to hover, as well as that it needs to be free from subjective, religious and commercial interests.

I am, of course, none the better. I always believed that an active democracy, where everybody has the right and the responsibility to vote on anything and everything, would be the ultimate answer. I even understood the challenge of the majority being affected by populism, which would ultimately lead voting power into becoming a winding fiasco. I have tried to envision that most people would be forced to learn from their mistakes, without acknowledging that that is often not the case.

First, lets talk about values. In a commercial reality, we have made the mistake of uplifting money to a value, maybe the value, while money is, and should always be, a tool to help us facilitate the true values in life. This misconception has turned into a kind of pervertism, which sucks any real value out of all life.

But let us return to the real values. What are needed are authentic all-governing values that stand above principles like the division of power between government, religion, police or any other system. The values cannot even be moral finger pointing, but have to be of the purest, highest aesthetics.

As stupid as it might sound, these values will be simple, like being nice to each other, using common sense and being humble with each other.

A society that puts such values above anything else will also let these values permeate through all the ladders of the population. The failure will slowly be turned into undivided success. Mark my words, those who show no fear, but dare to fight this way all the way through revolution, will also ensure the resolution and ultimate progress of civilisation."

Even though he sensed the world had tried not to let his words have meaning, they still made him proud. If all of his life would be a failure, this speech would become his legacy.

He should have noticed the first time, when she started to ask him about work. Not just the first time, but repeatedly with small, seemingly innocent prods. How easy it was for him to mistake it for honest interest. There was always that dangerous point in a relationship where the girl moves into a deeper personal level.

By hard-earned experience he knew that this was the moment, *el momento de verdad*, where time required him to call it off. If he let a woman get too close, there would be drama, tears and a hassle to get rid of her. He even credited himself with a set system where he knew exactly the actions to both postpone the moment and to elegantly break it off.

In reality, there never would be anything dignified about it. It was grim and strenuous, but compulsory to keep his personal failure at bay.

He should have noticed when she got them a spot at the best

restaurant in town, without a waiting list. Only people with power – lots of it – would be able to pull off such a feat.

He was too shallow and preferred to enjoy the food, the drinks and her too much to bother.

The royal family of Queen Cuisine and King Alcohol had become his best friends during the years. He spent hours every day savouring the gifts they provided him on this earth. Who needs three wise men anyway?

He shouldn't have ignored it when she was searching through his belongings when she thought him blind to other occupations. Again he wrongly credited it to her personal involvement. He silently started the preparation to give her the boot.

That's why he'd come here, to her place. Just to discover that the cards had been shuffled. How very irritating; he should have known better. Poker had never been his game. In some kind of perverted way he probably wanted to get caught, as some kind of escape, to help him out of the situation, as he never would be man enough to save himself.

The cigar-stenched man was obviously in charge; the skinnier bloke on his right, probably one of his Indians. She sat there as well, cold, but also hateful. Her eyes shone with freezing intensity. In the end, she had been a better actor than him. Envy and respect filled his return stare.

Did she understand? At least he saw something that could be the hint of surprise – but it may be that recognition existed purely in his fantasy.

He felt the flick and the expectation of triumph from the others, emanating like two radiant light bulbs. He felt no failure; curiosity owned him, the first occasion in which he had ever experienced such a thing.

Time to play his hand.

All his life he had been wondering if he enjoyed the deep flavours, relished from cigars. Today he knew the concluding answer.

"It must be similar to a good vintage wine, to sit there and harvest your prize. Unfortunately, I will have to disappoint you. You can show the pictures wherever you like, to whomever you like. I don't care. I might cheat on my wife, or kids or whatever, but I will never ever betray my country. Doesn't feel so sweet now, does it?"

Lost, astray and all alone

"Loneliness is strongest when experienced together, in silence."

Two excerpts from "The Lonely Travellers' Space Language":

1. "Tin licker: A person who solely drinks out of cans."
2. "Deaf grenade: Tin-can-based grenade with short-range sound and radio wave silence, made infamous by the McHannan Guerrilla."

It can be difficult to define what total darkness really is.

It is not the time when you are four years old and get caught by the elders in the act of stealing toys from your brother, and get your gruel as both of you have to watch the little toys – the toys you don't possess – disintegrate inside a simple open-fire device.

It is not the time when you were sixteen and your parents got murdered in front of your very eyes. Your elder brother being partly responsible flees the area and your life.

It is not the time your brother returns two years later to "rescue" you into a new profession consuming you into the grey days of piracy and shady deals.

It might be the time when a long line of assignments – which never actually brought you the kind of wealth you were dreaming of, but instead kept you in a fairly steady state of poverty – goes so totally wrong that your little excuse of a ship is torn to pieces and you are falling down into the atmosphere of a desolate and hostile planet. The ship is barely holding up; all systems, including life support, are about to fail. If you survive the landing, there is nowhere to go; you are all alone, alone in the vast, cold and harsh Universe.

But then again, the very nature of total in total darkness might implicate that it is a paradox and it can only exist on its own.

Pain, then light.

She is still alive; the ship still holds together, but the sounds, the hammering alarm of every system of the ship; failed or about to fail. What about life support? She tries to calm her panicking breathing when she discovers that there are only three minutes left and she already knows from scanning this planet, which doesn't even hold a proper name – just one of those numbers she can't even remember – that it is extremely toxic. Lethal. A place no organic matter wants ever to be.

A stressing calm fills her, only a fast resolution can save her life. Can she divert some power from other systems to life support? If only there was any power to divert. Is there some way she can scavenge parts of her own ship to re-establish a minimum of life support? She fails – horrendously – and when the minutes are up, she sits quietly – sobbing – with one of the external suits, which boosts its own life support for another four hours.

The ship is exhausted; everything turns black. It is dark, but not totally.

Maybe she will be able to re-wire a part of the transmission system so she can relay a distress signal? Of course, that might get her in the hands of her pursuers, but even that could bring a hope of extending her tiny excuse of a life.

She hates the fact that she is not very technically adept and most of the time she is pulling on wires, pushing buttons and admiring microchips without any clue of what she is doing. Should there not be an almost mechanical back-up system for distress signals on every ship by law? One of those laws that are common throughout the Empire, the Alliance and the Federation. Yes, it must be. But where is it?

Her eyes flicker through the transmission assets and there, easily spotted, she sees the unmistakable sign of emergency communication. It's a flash with a red diamond in the middle with the well-known exclamation marks forming an E, some of the more traditional and old-fashioned still refer to it as the S.O.S.

Desperate, as if there were not still three hours left, she breaks open the compartment, just to be greeted by the surprise of disappointment: a tin can with "Great Meatballs". Someone before her, obviously, had seen the need for these cheap, mystery meat treats as more important than saving her life here and now.

As reality sinks in, she realises there is no more hope. She decides she might as well have some fun. With a box of meatballs, she decides to leave the ship and enter a mighty three-hour adventure of a worthless planet.

Her mind denies the truth and hence, her mood rises.

She has become a great discoverer, one of the most famous ones. Her name is Vivian Lee and this planet is one of the greatest, a long-thought lost one, which now finally has been rediscovered and it will bear her name, gaining her immortality. It will be known as the planet that provided the Federation with such a great boost in rare resources that it will carry the name Vivally – which will be also known as praise to any girl – making a difference in a male-dominated world.

There is little light, but enough glimmering for her to know where to step and get a slight feel of direction. The surface is flat, boring, without any structures, as far as she can see. She does not mind, the exploration is more a fantasy within her head than anything else. When the oxygen runs out, she falls down on the ground perfectly happy in her mind. A good Vivallied way to die.

Darkness.

पूरस्वाप

No matter how many centuries the civilisations evolve, no matter what great inventions the geniuses inspire in our world, no matter how far we can reach, twist and manipulate outside and inside into the matters of existence, certain things seems to be incurable, like the existence of prostitutes or the fact that the larger part of any population struggles in their life below any defined poverty lines. Somehow, her brother, the three years older Jaz-Yn, was so lucky to receive a four-piece gift set of classic holo action figures. Even though it was probably already about a century old, it was still in reasonably good condition and worth something equal to a year's income for their family. How it had made its way into her brother's arms was unknown, but it filled her with devious envy. She had no concept of where this negativity of feelings came from; she knew just one thing: she wanted those holo figures.

The classic four-piece set was the one of the McHannan Guerrilla, which in its true existence had been a bloody fight for own-governing of immoveable-property rights gone sour – all too sour. But later, it had been turned into a heroic fairytale, which inspired youths across the fractions of space.

The first piece was that of Kez, the fiery one, the ginger head, the fighter and leader of men, women and children. Filled with a built-in hatred to anything controlled, anything unfair and with his built-in nonsense indicators of danger, which led him into more than a hundred documented deadly situations, just to survive into life as an old, grumpy and bitter man.

His brother, Timmie, the famous peacemaker, politician and diplomat. Even though sources later indicated that Timmie could have been a rotten apple, most people held a lot of esteem to such a man and stories would tell that even in the most diabolical of hells, he did keep honour, respect and honesty as his deepest virtues.

The guerilla princess, Slyane, rumoured to be so beautiful that most men who laid eyes up on her would be stunned by her beauty, just to end up dead in the next moment. Both McHannan brothers loved her – deeply – it was this love that in the end broke the spell of virtue. Timmie ran away with her and Kez fought the remaining years as a sad and bitter leader.

The little, playful, young boy, Beeze, who in many ways was more of a helper and assistant. In later years after the fall of Kez and the end of the conflict, he rose to become an official leader and icon of a better world.

Each piece by its own had one story to tell, of their individual figure. But it was when they were connected together that their capabilities shone and additional stories unlocked, those classic fairytales, remodelled and remade, brimmed up with morals and ethics to be suitable for little children.

She was only four and she got caught red-handed by her mother, during her silly theft; it was not nice. Both of them were forced to look at the flames when the holo figures were burned in the small open-fire device. A fortune, in value, but also one of the few toys they ever possessed, blazing into oblivion.

Something in the invincible lines of the relationship within the family was also cremated that day.

पूरस्वाप

Pain, light, a little noise.

Is she dead? Is she alive? She feels her own body, the space suit. Her eyes open; there is such a bright light. She is lying on the ground and the pain is still her friend. Some of the older space suits had a flaw in them – one of the kind she was wearing – that when it ran out of power, some small valves would no longer be tight. As they were put out of production, they were sold cheap in the second-hand market and therefore their use was quite widespread in the galaxies.

It meant that this planet was breathable. It meant a new chance to live.

It meant that the computer archive of her ship, of most ships, was incorrect, but why? Not the right moment to think about it. Now, this can of less-quality meat would be a delight. All suits also had a small reserve of water, so she could sit down on the dry ground and enjoy the feast of a meatballs and water breakfast, a Sunday picnic on a planet of no choice.

She did need to get more food and water though, now she needed to return to the ship. But she no longer had any sense of direction on which way to head and the surface she travelled on was too hard to keep any clues.

She made her best guess and let luck decide the outcome, but fortune did not play on her side. The little reserve of energy built up from the meal was seeping out of her like a hole in an old dam. Without noticing it, she went from stable back into her fantasy of the planet Vivally. Into a state of hallucinations and babbling. A knight of her order, with a crescent-mooned cape, was approaching, jumped off his horse and greeted her.

"Dr Vivian Lee, I presume?"

Then she fell, exhausted, and fainted. And she was back into the black.

पूरसूवाप

As a consequence of the McHannan Guerilla fighting for their rights across a whole solar system and winning, its members became popular among common people and some even adopted the McHannan name to pretend they were in direct relation.

So it was with De'Cris McHannan, the foreigner that utilised his claimed legacy, supplemented with nice words of freedom fighting, as a platform to promote his own crime syndicate – one that expanded faster than photons.

Even though he never got to play with the hologram toys, he knew the stories like the back of his hand. De'Cris was like his long-lost brother, a friend, a treasure that he had been seeking all his life. Although he was barely a man, he became a fierce freedom fighter, which in reality was the building blocks of his doom.

His parents did not understand either, only she did. She could contemplate behind the lies; recognise the increase of drugs on the streets.

Society could not in any way tolerate that he controlled sixty per cent of the city's revenue. The retaliation was swift and ruthless. Armed forces bringing down the new mafia cartel in high style.
It was the biggest bust ever and her brother was about to be jailed or killed in the attempt. She never knew the consequences when she, in deep desperation, rat on him to her origin.

They, of course, wanted to save him, the elder brother, the upcoming man of the family. In the heat that followed there were no more elders, a fugitive brother with his brother from another mother, and her, all alone.

Despair, loneliness and tears were her only friends now.

पूरस्वाप

But death did not fit her; again she woke up to light, but this time inside a dwelling. The moon knight had not been a fantasy. The planet was inhabited, although the person that gazed about her while she lay helpless on the divan was a poor excuse to turn a hostile planet into a home. Somehow she was wondering if her mind was lost and she was just imagining stuff, one vision more fantastic than the other.

The terrible aftertaste of the "Great Meatballs", the mystery meat of survival, was too intense for this to be her own personal state of madness.

"Who are you?"

She spoke fast and insecurely, like someone pushed into a corner with no way out. He could not care less, spoke and moved slowly, like a world second-hand in motion.

"It has been a long time since anybody has asked me this. Truly, names have no meaning for me any more. If you like, you can call me anything."

"This is stupid; everybody has a name. What was the name you used to have?"

"I will not go by that name any more."

"Then what will I call you?"

"Anything you like."

"My God, you are irritating."

"Maybe a thanks, for saving your life, would be in order?"

She was furious inside; who did this guy think he was? Some kind of funny Joe, who could behave rudely in any situation?

"Thank you."

This was the start of a challenging and difficult conversation; she almost exploded from frustration, but somehow, his pace, the place, the emptiness, it all got to her and she managed to abstain from strangling the stranger.

The small cottage had two rooms only, dug into some natural rocky material with a white cottonish glow. The kitchen corner was loaded with what seemed to be an endless rack of tin cans – food, but no meatballs.

If he told the truth, something that could be doubtful, then she had learned the following: they were the only people on this planet. This was the only building and there was nothing to really do there, except eat, drink and sleep; not much different from life in general. But life in general would become extremely boring already after two days.

She had no idea, why he was there, what he was doing there and how he had got there. And she really had no clue as to why she was there either; nothing really gave any meaning. Yes, there had been occasions when the star maps were incorrect, but whenever the fault was as big as a whole planet, something or someone else usually was involved. Some conspiracy of any kind. But this man was not such.

The food was stale; it was boxed. Even though she had the choice of different meals, it all tasted the same. Her tastebuds were not eloquent enough to differentiate the alleged non-gourmet variety. The only thing to drink was also whatever the cans provided – nice stuff – but eventually, boring as well. It was like everything around here promoted one thing only: the luxuries of apathy.

She could feel – deep inside of her – that something was really, really wrong. As boredom struck her and he was somewhere out of sight, she started to look for something to do. From a shelf something struck her hard in the head.

"The classic game of 'Q-bomb or peace'."

And of course, out of nowhere he came as he was somehow magically watching her every step.

"Yes, and so what?"

"Well, if you are looking for something to pass time, as this seems to be one of the things that bother you, my guess is that life outside this planet did not leave you with much time for such pleasures. Your real issue is most likely that you never had any time to spend to enjoy and therefore ultimately ended up in doldrums."

He talked a lot, maybe it made sense, but she could not fathom it.

"Ok, let's play, I will be the good gal."

"You do not realise that in the original game design, the good guys and gals actually existed, but due to the potential lesser sales by addressing any of the large fractions of space as bad guys, it was left out. Funny thing is that with the clever new design, they actually made the game, not just a fling thing, but an instant classic, one of these games everybody has, but grows tired of in their teens."

"I never had it, but have played it a lot when I was younger."

"It still proves my point; the actual design where you can choose to be either the Federation, the Empire, the Alliance or the Consortium of non-human races, it reflects the real world more precisely."

"What do you mean?"

"In the real world, none of the Fractions really are the bad or the good guys; everywhere in the world you will find both. However, just like in the game, they all have their advantages and weaknesses."

"What about the animals? That kind of breaks your theory of realism."

"Hah, just because we do not know about them any more, doesn't mean the non-human races never existed."

He left again and she was abandoned to play the game all by herself. The words, the inner meaning of what had not been spoken; his sentences taunted her, while she put in a victory for the non-humans.

पूरस्वाप

Time – this very substance, so fragile, so important to us humans, but so utterly disregarded from the massive mechanisms, the bowl of juice, that recipe that makes up the very Universe, the very life we live – unfolded itself at a tiresome pace.

A pace she could not stand – it was not only the bore – seconds that never seemed to move to the next. Also the thoughts, lingering worries, the slow deduction process of what had happened previous to her entering this planet – she now only knew as Vivally, the nameless one had somehow silently agreed on the name – and all that had transpired here haunted her.

In the years she had stayed alone, she had been forced to commit to the most unworthy of acts to survive. She would rather forget, but the feeling in the flesh would and could never heal. She would never be whole again. Somehow her brother had come back to her. "Saving her to the revolution." as he would boast. Even though she knew the truth behind the layer of lies, even though she never could forgive him for the parents' deaths, she let herself fall back, bending over to the lies, as it was still an opening for a better life.

She was caught into something different, into a life promising the dream of that one golden job that could make them – make her – rich, prosperous enough to really live, a life without sorrows but with limitless joys. For some reason, it seemed that any job they did, any task she accomplished somehow dug her deeper into the McHannan well of debt.

It was never really bad, it was by far the best days of her life until this day. Here though, she was in utter unease by the setting. Was this reality or had she somehow turned mad? A man without a name, a planet with her name, with only two persons, habitable but boring.

A very unlikely case for reality, the chance of this oddness to be true would probably be less than winning the first price in The Federation Lottery. And yet here she was. The food tasted real, the smells, although oddly unknown, seemed genuine. But could she really trust it? Trust her own judgement?

Her baffling concern fought her, while she played Q-bomb or peace, initially she preferred to win by the Q-bomb, but over time she found more satisfaction in the peaceful victory. It was simply harder to accomplish.

Every morning he would leave, to whatever joy he found in the harsh landscape, only to return for a less-than-lovely tinned dinner. They would converse, but she would never get anywhere with him; it was like there was no progress and any chat would be similar to their first.

One day, alone, she bumped into a tower of cans, only to discover something strange behind them, something like rock-clad discs with strange, carved, round patterns.

Even more peculiar was the device, which seemed to fit the shellac discs. She hovered down to it to take a closer look, just to find words streaming into her ear. Again he was there, as if he knew everything she did.

"It's a relic from the old days, from the Sol System, in the early days of humans, when they just discovered how to transform sound into storage to play back at any other time."

He passed her, and showed her how to turn it on. Sound poured through the rooms.

"It sounds like noise to me."

"Ah, but it's so much the opposite, unlike the over-processed frequencies you normally refer to as music, this is the pure sound of instruments, the tools of music recorded in pure material to preserve the essence of the original performed piece."

"Yeah right, like your nice words can ever make this sound anything else than random irritating screeches."

The passiar was over, but she kept interest in the turntable, for no other reason than another utility to pass time. The sound somehow soothed the negative thought patterns and put her at ease.
And as days passed, the noise turned into music, vibrating her bones into emotions.

On several days he would return home to find her crying, without any clear reason.

And somehow the time turned from boredom to joy. Somehow she started smiling and their conversations became long and wonderful. They could stay up late at night and talk for hours. She told her story and he listened.

He never talked about himself, but told her about the world, about the Universe, about all the things she never had had the chance to see. The beauty of a falling star or a star born.

It was like life slowly became a fairytale and she was the princess in it.

But obviously it could not last.

पूरस्वाप

She was lying down, just letting the ancient tunes play with her and trying to suppress the growing hate to having every meal and drink served from a tin can, when fate again played with her and the planet was not the place for two sole occupants any more.

The room, filled up with ghosts of her past. De'Cris McHannan and a bunch of his henchmen – but not her brother – armed to the teeth, surrounding her in contrast to the tunes, as a treat. A death treat.
She was tired, so tired of death lingering between every corner. So tired of life playing its notorious games with her as a pawn and being pushed to the very edge of life itself. She decided to play the hopeless-and-stupid card.

"De'Cris, you found me."
"Of course I did, you still owe me what I need."
"I am so happy to see you, but I am so very sorry that the cargo got lost. There were so many after it, at least two or three other groups, all attacking at once. At least the cargo ship blew up in the heat, so nobody else got it either."

Surprisingly, the room was filled with the laughter of the claim-to-be McHannan; its rolling sound was about as pleasant as a meat grinder on speed.

"You stupid woman, you always carried the cargo yourself."
"What do you mean? I don't understand."
"The real cargo was deep-level, highly sensitive, very secret information coded into nanobots and injected into your body."
"What?"
"However, you do not have to be alive for us to retrieve it and I prefer you dead this time, to prevent you from another failure of a mission."
"What about my brother?"
"He already believes you're dead, let's keep it that way. Guys, let's finish her."

Her enemies were many, over equipped with the latest of protective gear, communication equipment and arms. It was a match to make, she stood no chance, had no way of surviving this time, and there would not be any easy way out.

She did a surprise jump to the side, diagonally across towards De'Cris himself. Caught by the moment, he did not have time to react before an open tin can cut him in the face.

And that was all she could do before she got hit hard and everything became black and she descended onto the floor.

पूरस्वाप

Her brother, eager, told her that this was the job, the one to bring them cash in such amounts that they could live happily ever after. Still, it was only a small-risk job because only a selected few knew about the cargo run and her job would be to escort it to ensure successful delivery. She had asked why such value would be escorted by her little ship; her questions were brushed off with the reason of keeping the transport discreet.

But once she was on the run, there was nothing discreet about it; several fractions with large ships, a rather heavy arsenal of guns all wanted the cargo.

And little did she know, she was the carrier.

पूरस्वाप

Before De'Cris could finish her off there was the distinct sound of a hard metal object hitting the floor, stealing the attention from everybody in the room. And then there was only silence, no more communication; total. A deaf grenade, a whirlwind, a shadow that entered the room, travelling like a hidden ninja between the thugs, finishing them off in perfect matter. The bodies falling to the floor, one by one, almost like in a slow-motion sequence without the usual foley. No one had a chance, not even De'Cris.

This was possibly the first time in history that the bumpy rides of the reels of T-Bone Walker's Lollie Lou has created absolutely no sound at all. "Please listen to my song. Come back where you belong."

पूरस्वाप

What kind of joke it was that the gods played with her was unknown, but somehow she arose to consciousness yet again, lying on a straw mat in some sort of cave. A rich plant and flower life blooming in thousands of colours and smells around her. And the man – who would like to have no name – was hovering above her.

"There you are, back to life."
"Where are we?"
"Under the planet crust. I think it is time to show you the truth."
"Truth?"
"Come on, you did not really believe at any point that the cottage was the premises of this planet."
"You tricked me?"
"Not really, on the surface that is the only liveable place, but here, below, I have created a beautiful world, full of life and wonder."
"But why?"
"Let's begin with who, shall we?"
"Who?"
"I am Kez McHannan."
"I wonder what drugs you are on, Kez lived ages ago, he is dead."
"You know very well that nano technology can makes wonders to

your life span."

"Still, there are limits to it."

"Not really, the limits you know about are implied limits, created limits to prevent people from living forever, but with the right amount of money and technology, there are no limits. Not any more."

"Even if I would believe you, you do not have the right hair colour."

"True, I changed my appearance as well, otherwise about every citizen of this Universe would recognise me."

"On a deserted planet?"

"Well, it was before I moved here."

"I am full of doubt, but tell me your story."

"You see, I believed in the cause, what we fought for. I thought of myself as a good man, a man with values. But in reality I was a brute, a brute that was used; we all were used as a part of the global greed for resources."

"What do you mean?"

"You see, we were not really an independent group fighting for freedom, because we were secretly founded by an opposing organisation, whose interest was to get their hands on the resources, especially minerals and rare metals from the planets, and they figured the best way to do so was masked as a support to a group of fighters: us. It all boils down to the eternal fight of resources, which is again triggered by the eternal fight to use, abuse, buy, build and sell more and more things, equipment, tools, furniture, anything, to trigger even more greed, more things. And yes, this does have the side effect that it creates a richer world, which in turn triggers more people with greed for more things, and more resources have to be depleted to feed the never-ending hunger for more. In this game, which can benefit some, but in reality, it just uses the same, it uses anyone or anything, to keep feeding itself, and in turn I lost my family and the girl I loved. And in the years after, I finally understood it. Like a sad and wiser man."

"And then you magically transferred from there to here?"

"Ah, it's more to it than that; it is amazing what you can do when you twist the arm that feeds you. My secret plan, at that time the idea was just to get away – to live in solace and repent – unfolded and I set up the beginning of this planet. But over time, I have grown and created this wonderful world, hidden from the world above, and I think maybe one day it will be time to reveal it for the world, but only for the ones that need it, which are pure, like you."

"Like shit, I am not pure at all, you should know that."

"Yes, maybe not, but you are still pure at heart, that much I know, and in the end, that's what counts."

"Then I think the time is now."

"No, no, there is still so much to do, so many things I need to get done..."

He stopped his rambling when he saw her deep, accusing eyes.

"Maybe you are right, maybe it's time. First, let's have a look at what's hiding inside of you."

They both smiled in a relaxed and beautiful way – the first time of many.

Some words by the author:

When I finished my debut tetralogy in Norwegian, my plan was to have a pause from writing, maybe even an infinite pause. But faith had other plans for me and at the end of the year 2013 I met a girl during lunch who invited me to join a writing group that wrote short stories in English. Having tried my first English short story earlier as a part of Elite: Chronicles (which was to be an official Elite: Dangerous release, but for various reasons was never finished), I was eager to continue in this direction, but most of all, I was in need of a challenge.

Being part of such a group was a very good learning experience for me – the vast difference between the writers, the direct, but polite feedback knocking you where it hurts the most, where it is needed the most. But more importantly, the inspiration it gave me, inspiration to redefine within myself what a story is, and how to approach the art of conveying this to you. I have as such reduced my sexual, violent and crazy style, to focus on actually being able to write in a non-native language as well as to train in the technique of storytelling. Still, you will recognise my own style and technique all the way from beginning to end, resulting in something unique but still something broader, something that can be a provocation as well as a treasure in your own living adventure.

Returning feedback from the group from almost every story

you can find in this book was that they wanted more, that I could expand on each storyto become a whole book. Now that was the kind of feedback that made my heart *flutter*, but the fact is, except for two (!) stories about Kenneth Johansen, these stories are written to be standalone, and never (say never agian) anything more.

This book, as an outcome of the challenge, is meant as a teaser, a taste of what I might be able to cook up in the future. Will it be more of Kenneth Johansen's not so good detective work or will it be something entirely different? We will see.

If you like this book, do not hesitate to write an online review, recommend it to family and friends, tweet it and even post pictures of you reading it. Feedback is of course also appreciated (don_chand@chasvag.com).

I wish you the best of luck.
Chand Svare Ghei

About the author:

Chand Svare Ghei (1976) is a leading IT and telecommunications engineer. He has an extremely broad experienced background including time spent in Afghanistan, Kosovo and Bosnia.

He has written his books in more than twenty countries and he uses reality as his main inspiration as he feels that reality provides even better stories than fantasy. This is the reason why the world he pens is close to ours, but contains various mysterious deviations.

In his early years, his mother introduced him to the world of fiction. This was the beginning of his love for creating short stories. For much of his childhood and youth years he continued writing until an abrupt pause when he reached his twenties. Life demanded other things from him.

Until 2004, when he was travelling to some of the most romantic locations on earth, he was again convinced under a shining moon to re-enter the worlds created by queues of letters. He had a dream to fulfill.

www.ingramcontent.com/pod-product-compliance
Lightning Source LLC
Chambersburg PA
CBHW020343260626
47156CB00004B/1665